'Not in a milli

Clancy leapt to her
any woman you ch
little finger, but I'r
harem—and I never

A mocking smile curved Luke's mouth. 'You would have appeared to have thrown down a gauntlet, Clancy. And in public, too.' His dark eyes glinted dangerously. 'So perhaps you should know—I never refuse a challenge.'

Dear Reader

Over the past year, along with our usual wide variety of exciting romances, you will, we hope, have been enjoying a romantic journey around Europe with our Euromance series. From this month, you'll be able to have double the fun and double the passion, as there will now be two Euromance books each month—one set in one of your favourite European countries, and one on a fascinating European island. Remember to pack your passport!

The Editor

When **Rachel Elliot** was a child in Aberdeen, she was frequently to be found comfortably perched in the branches of an apple tree, scribbling stories. Now she lives in the beautiful Borders, and she's still scribbling—but now from an office overlooking the stable yard of her small pony-trekking centre. She's crazy about animals, as you'd see from her motley collection of four-legged and feathered friends. Oh, yes—she also works as a reporter/presenter with Border Television. Life certainly isn't boring!

Recent titles by the same author:

UNWANTED LEGACY

RESCUED

BY

RACHEL ELLIOT

MILLS & BOON LIMITED
ETON HOUSE,   18-24 PARADISE ROAD
RICHMOND,   SURREY   TW9 1SR

First published in Great Britain 1993
by Mills & Boon Limited

© Rachel Elliot 1993

Australian copyright 1993
Philippine copyright 1993
This edition 1993

ISBN 0 263 78224 7

Set in Times Roman 10½ on 12 pt.
01-9309-48343 C

Made and printed in Great Britain

CHAPTER ONE

CLANCY heaved a sigh that seemed to have come from the soles of her elegantly though not very comfortably shod feet. Would this journey never end? Whoever it was that had said ' 'Tis better to travel hopefully than to arrive' had obviously never driven from London to Cumbria, she reflected grouchily, raising one hand from the steering-wheel to rub her eyes wearily. In truth, though, she couldn't blame her tiredness on the journey alone. Its roots went back further than that.

Barely managing to stifle a yawn, she glanced with little hope at the road ahead, praying for some sign of a service station or café. A cup of coffee would give a much needed boost to her flagging energy right about now. Instead, all she could see was scenery—endless vistas of dramatic hills and glistening waters, the beautiful unrivalled scenery that only the Lake District could offer, but totally wasted on her at that precise moment.

Well, it was her own fault. She should have stuck to the motorway instead of giving in to that insistent inner voice telling her she should be starting to absorb the feelings and atmosphere of this new and alien land.

She gave a start, her pulse racing alarmingly as she realised her thoughts had been wandering. As tired as she was, she couldn't afford to lose concentration now. Just a few more miles and she could book into the hotel, immerse herself in a soothing hot bath, then crawl between welcoming sheets. The prospect shimmered tantalisingly before her like a mirage in a desert and unthinkingly she closed her eyes.

The sudden harsh blaring of a car horn blasted its way into her fuddled brain, and acting entirely on instinct she slammed her foot hard on the brake, her heart hammering painfully within her chest as the car slewed to a halt. For a long moment she could only sit there, recovering from the shock, trying to understand what had happened. Then a shadow fell on the side-window.

'What the hell do you think you're playing at?' Even through the glass she could hear the irate note in his voice. 'You were wandering about all over the road—one second more and you'd have been on the other side of the carriageway altogether.'

She took a deep breath, keeping her eyes downward as she wound down the window.

'I'm sorry,' she said at last. 'My mind must have wandered for a moment.'

'Wandered?' He gave a harsh bark of laughter. 'Lady, you fell asleep at the wheel! You could have killed yourself—not to mention any other poor unsuspecting travellers who had the misfortune to chance into your path.'

She knew he was only speaking the truth, but a combination of guilt and annoyance at his arrogant manner made her bridle.

'Now wait just a minute!' She tilted her chin defiantly as she finally raised her eyes to meet his, only to find her words dying on her lips. Looked as if the old Clancy J. Hall talent for bad timing was still holding good, she reflected with an inner irony she could only pray wouldn't show on her normally all too expressive face. Just her luck to come face to face with the most devastatingly gorgeous man she'd ever seen, in circumstances like these.

Not that she had either need or desire for any member of the male species right now, no matter how gorgeous, she reminded herself hurriedly—but still, it was somewhat galling to look into eyes so deep and dark and see only scorn and anger there.

'Well?'

'Well?' She gazed back at him uncomprehendingly and his mouth tightened.

'You asked me to wait a minute,' he said, his voice heavily laden with sarcasm. 'I'm still waiting.'

Since whatever biting comment she'd been preparing to deliver had completely deserted her memory, she could only blink helplessly, feeling uncharacteristically floored. Where was her much lauded talent for always having an answer for everything now, when she really needed it?

The man gave an impatient grunt. 'Get out of the car,' he ordered tersely.

'I beg your pardon?' Her eyes widened in stunned amazement. Just who did he think he was, issuing commands like that? He was obviously well accustomed to being in charge of things, she realised, but that didn't give him the right to start ordering her about.

'You heard. Get out of the blasted car.'

'I'll do no such thing.' If she'd been standing up she'd have planted both hands on her hips—as it was, the only thing she could do was glare balefully back at him. To her annoyance she saw a glint of amusement in his dark smoky grey eyes. 'For all I know you could be planning to steal my car and leave me stranded here.'

'If you'd care to glance in your rear-view mirror you'll see I already possess a car,' he returned patiently.

And not just any old car either, but a gleaming, lovingly maintained Morgan. A car that no one in his right mind would want to swap for her battered old work-horse of a Mini, much though it pained her to admit it.

'Now get out of the car.'

'No.'

She could see he was working hard to rein in his anger and it sent a shiver of apprehension right through her. This was not a man to tangle with—even though that beautifully constructed body barely con-fined within well-worn jeans and faded denim shirt had doubtless tempted countless women to tangle to their hearts' content. Bemused by the sudden wayward path her thoughts were taking, she scowled up at him as though he was to blame.

'You might be planning to abduct me.'

This time there was no mistaking his amusement as his lips quirked mirthfully. 'Lady, the way I feel right now I'd rather horsewhip you. Now get out of the car!'

Measuring all of five feet three in her socks and with a build that could best be described as slender, it was still a rare event when Clancy J. Hall was forced to admit she'd met her match. But this was one of those times, much as it rankled to accept the unpalatable fact. It was only because she was so bone-weary, she told herself—normally she'd have matched him word for blistering word. She'd been accused in the past of never knowing when to give in gracefully, even when the odds were stacked against her. Now, though, she was all too aware that the fight had drained out of her normally feisty spirit, leaving her with no choice. Sighing heavily, she released the seatbelt and climbed from the driver's seat.

'OK, you win. Now what?' Her wide-set hazel eyes narrowed suspiciously as she looked up at him, feeling at no greater advantage now she was standing before him, her diminutive figure dwarfed by his tall, powerful frame.

He folded his arms and leaned casually back against the car, a cool breeze ruffling his thick mane of jet-black hair. 'Start breathing in some of this good fresh air,' he said.

'Why?'

'To help you wake up.'

'What makes you think I'm tired?'

She knew she was verging on being childish, but having given in to him once simply made her all the more determined to dig her heels in now.

His eyes raked over her features ruthlessly and she suffered under his scrutiny.

'You look as if you haven't slept in a week,' he said bluntly. 'You've got shadows like bruises under your eyes and your skin's as white as a sheet. You look like a wreck. Unless that's what you normally look like, of course, in which case you've got real problems.'

'Gee, thanks.' She was irritated to discover just how much his comments hurt. She'd never suffered under any delusions of beauty, it was true, but her heart-shaped face with its huge hazel eyes, tip-tilted nose and boyishly cropped auburn hair had never been described as a wreck before.

'Why didn't you simply pull into a lay-by and grab a nap?'

Her answering look registered astonishment that such a question could even be asked.

'Here? In the middle of nowhere? What do you think I am—crazy?'

'Let's leave my assessment of your mental state out of this for the moment, since you probably wouldn't appreciate it much,' he returned calmly. 'But since you were clearly out on your feet, it surely would have made sense to stop for a while.'

Unthinkingly she shook her head. 'Too risky,' she muttered.

It was his turn to look surprised. 'Risky?' he echoed. 'In the middle of the Lake District?'

'You think just because this place is wild and beautiful it doesn't have its share of nutcases just waiting to pounce on the defenceless?' Her eyes shot sparks as she glowered angrily up at him. 'Which for all I know could be a perfect description of you!'

'Lady, in the short space of time I've known you, I've come to the conclusion that no one in their right mind could describe you as defenceless.' He paused, his eyes narrowing thoughtfully as he scrutinised her features. She looked away, made strangely uncomfortable by his penetrating gaze, then flinched violently as he reached out a hand to cup her chin, the warmth of his fingers sending an unaccountable jolt throughout her system.

'How dare you?' She wrenched violently away from his grasp, her eyes seeming larger than ever as she backed away from him. 'You have no right to…to…'

'To touch you?'

She nodded, horribly aware that her reaction had been excessive. Now he really would think she was crazy.

'I don't like being touched by strangers,' she said stiltedly.

'Why not?'

Her eyes flew back to his face. What was this—an inquisition?

'Why do you want to know?' she hedged.

'Why don't you want to tell me?' he countered swiftly.

Once again she was left floundering. This man was impossible. He'd met her just a few moments ago, albeit not in the most happy of circumstances, and seemed to think he had the right to her life story.

'Because I don't like being questioned . . .'

'By strangers.' He finished the sentence for her, his dark grey eyes narrowing assessingly. 'So tell me, how do you ever manage to make friends?'

Tired as she was, she felt a spurt of anger flaring up inside her.

'Friends?' she echoed incredulously. 'Friends? You've already managed to insinuate I'm crazy and you've told me I look a wreck. Surely you can't expect me to harbour any friendly feelings towards you after that inauspicious start?'

His massive shoulders lifted fractionally in a shrug. 'Real friends don't pussyfoot round the truth,' he said shortly. 'No matter how much it hurts.'

She looked down at the ground, restlessly scuffing her elegant court shoe in the gravel. 'That may be true of your friends,' she said sullenly. 'I prefer mine to be a little more circumspect.'

'Then they're nothing more than acquaintances.' A lock of hair fell forward into his eyes as he shook his head. He raked it impatiently back and her eyes were riveted to the sight of his long tanned fingers pushing their way through the thick waves, only now spotting the silver strands sprinkled among the black. Suddenly she found herself wondering about him—she'd been stunned by the sheer male beauty of the man on first seeing him. Now, on closer study, she could see there was a great deal more to him than simple good looks.

His features might originally have been bestowed upon him by a beneficent maker, but he clearly hadn't wrapped that glorious frame in cotton wool. His eyes, dark and smoky grey, held shadows that could only have been put there by painful experience, a pain that was echoed in the lines harshly etched on his face. His nose, probably once classically perfect, had ob-

viously been broken at some stage, yet its slightly
squint look only added to the overall strength of what
was already a strong, uncompromising face.

Lost in musing contemplation of his features, she
dropped her eyes to his mouth, horrified when a shiver
rippled through her veins. His was a mouth created
for issuing commands, its lines stern and determined—yet faint traces etched at the corners showed
his capacity for laughter too. And there was more to
that mouth—much, much more. Inexperienced as she
was in the ways of love, the woman in her was drawn
inexorably to the sheer sensuality of those firm lips.
To be touched by them, to feel them against her own—
she closed her eyes, swaying slightly as a devastating
moment of longing coursed through her entire being.

Suddenly she gave an outraged squawk as she was
scooped unceremoniously into the air, then dumped
none too gently on the ground, firm fingers at the
back of her neck pushing her head forward between
her knees.

'What do you think you're doing?' Her words were
muffled in the material of her skirt.

'You were about to faint.' Apparently realising she
was in danger of suffocating, he pulled her skirt up
over her knees and she gasped in indignation.

'How dare you? I was not about to faint!'

'Lady, I've seen enough women on the verge of
having the vapours to recognise the signs. Now keep
your head down and take deep breaths.'

Even as she struggled against the cool fingers
holding her captive, she was gripped by a ridiculous
urge to giggle, tinged though it was by irritation. On

the verge of having the vapours, was she? He made
her sound like some Victorian miss in need of a strong
male hand. Well, that probably just about summed
up his attitude to women. He was clearly a chauvinist
of the worst kind, she decided, at the same time
worryingly aware that a maverick part of her supposedly liberated soul was actually enjoying the unaccustomed submissive role he was making her play.
It was that realisation that finally made her find suf-
ficient strength to twist savagely away from his con-
straining fingers. So he thought her a helpless woman,
did he? Then he didn't know Clancy J. Hall at all!

'I'll thank you to keep your hands to yourself.' She
scrambled to her feet, her hazel eyes shooting sparks
of fire. 'Just look what you've done to my clothes—
I look as though I've been rolling around in the dust.'

His eyes glinted as they swept over her, taking in
the crumpled linen skirt. 'Not quite the bandbox per-
fection your London acquaintances are accustomed
to seeing, I take it?'

She opened her mouth to give him a blistering
retort, then closed it again abruptly, her expression
curious. 'What makes you so sure I come from
London?'

He shook his dark head. 'I don't believe you come
from London,' he countered. 'There's just a hint of
accent left in your voice that didn't start off life in
the Smoke. But I'd hazard a guess that you live there.
Probably have done for some time. You've got that
city veneer.'

'I suppose you prefer your women with a healthy
country glow—all pink-cheeked and full of mother's

RESCUED   15

cooking.' She could have bitten her tongue out as soon
as she'd said the words, but it was too late. He was
clearly amused.

'At this early stage of our acquaintance I'd hardly
have described you as one of "my women",' he
drawled lazily. 'Still, if you'd like to apply...' He let
his words tail off as his eyes roamed indolently over
her body.

'I'd rather walk barefoot through a pit of rattle-
snakes,' she hissed back at him. 'At least in the city
men have manners, unlike you, you big country oaf.'

He tilted his head to one side, pretending to consider her words. 'Men with manners,' he said slowly.
'Yes, I have heard such a breed exists. What the glossy
magazines would describe as the "new man", I believe. Am I correct?'

She nodded warily, perfectly aware that a trap was
being set for her, but completely at a loss to know
how she could avoid it. 'That's right,' she said defiantly. 'The type of man who isn't afraid to show
emotion. The type of man who'll help out around the
house and take on his share of the domestic
responsibilities.'

An ironic grin lifted the corners of his mouth. 'Is
that really the sort of man city women want nowadays?' The dark eyes bored into her own. 'Is it the
sort of man you want?' He took a step towards her
and she moved hastily back, only to come up against
the solid, unmoving bulk of the car. Cornered, she
stood her ground, her chin tilting mutinously.

'That's typical of you,' she said scornfully. 'To simply dismiss a man strong enough to admit to his own vulnerabilities.'

His eyes glinted dangerously as he loomed over her. 'Don't you think it's a little presumptuous of you to decide what's "typical" of me after knowing me for such a short time?' he said in a voice that was quiet yet shot through with steel.

Feeling decidedly vulnerable herself, she strove to make her voice sound contemptuously dismissive. 'I'm a good judge of character. I can usually sum people up pretty accurately quite quickly.'

'Really? And how would you sum me up?'

'You're a stereotype. Mr Macho. A modern-day caveman.' She knew she was asking for trouble, deliberately courting it, yet she was unable to stop herself, finding some perverse pleasure in taunting him.

His eyes darkened. 'So I'm a caveman?' he said softly. 'Then I mustn't disappoint your expectations.'

'I have no...' But her voice died away as he swiftly closed the small gap between them, and before she had time to fully realise what was happening he had her ensnared in a vice-like grip, his arms tight about her squirming body.

'Let go of me!'

It didn't help her state of mind at all to realise that a tiny, renegade part of her soul wanted this craziness to continue—wanted to savour being in this man's strong embrace. His arms were firm against her back, pinioning her arms to her sides as he slid one hand upwards to cup the back of her neck. Then her eyes widened to their fullest extent as his other hand clamped over her backside, then lifted her clean off her feet.

Her indignant exclamation was smothered as his mouth claimed hers. For a moment she was too shell-shocked to react at all. Then to her fury she found her body was responding to him, her lips parting of their own accord, her hands clenching the material of his shirt. Appalled at having to fight herself as well as him, she began to struggle wildly, feeling his laughter reverberate through his chest.

'Careful, sweetheart,' he murmured against her mouth. 'Don't wriggle too much—I might just like it.'

'You're nothing but a ... a ...'

'A caveman?' His breath, warm and minty, caressed her fevered skin. 'So you've already said. So it seems to me that, since your mind's already well and truly made up, I might as well enjoy the role.'

His kiss was devastating, burning through the layers of her resistance, dissolving what little was left of her will to fight. His mouth moving relentlessly over her own managed to be both tender and totally domi-nating at one and the same time and she groaned helplessly, caught up in the grip of something she'd never experienced before. If her hands had been free to move, they'd have been clutching at his powerful body, pushing restlessly past the barrier of his shirt to reach the warm, vital skin beneath. As it was, even the thought of touching him more intimately was enough to send her senses reeling.

It was he who finally chose to end the kiss, setting her back on her feet with an arrogantly satisfied smile that instantly refuelled all the befuddled fury in her soul. Common sense driven from her, she lifted her hand to strike him, consumed by a need to obliterate the memory of her body's treachery in responding as it had. It was a futile gesture. Even as her fist flew through the air, he caught her wrist easily.

'I don't think so,' he said in a soft voice that sent shivers down her spine. 'Don't start something you can't hope to carry through to the finish. Otherwise you might find yourself taking on more than you can handle.'

'You may be physically stronger than me, but that doesn't make you a superior being.' She spat the words at him, incensed by her own impotence. 'What does brawn amount to? Nothing.'

'Then why did you attempt to hit me just now?' he returned easily, clearly enjoying himself. 'It seems you're not averse to resorting to physical retaliation yourself.'

'Only because you drove me to it.'

'Come, come.' He eyed her mockingly. 'Search your soul, little miss London. I think you'll find I did only what you wanted me to do.'

She turned away from his searching eyes, horribly aware that he was speaking no more than the truth. She had wanted him—with a blind, unreasoning need that swept all else from her mind. The anger she was feeling now should be aimed at herself as much as him.

'I'm leaving,' she said abruptly. 'Thank you for your assistance in preventing a possible accident.'

If he heard the sarcasm in her voice he gave no sign of it. 'You're welcome.'

Without as much as a backward glance she climbed into the car and closed the door firmly behind her. The sound of his soft laughter set her teeth on edge, but she resolutely ignored it, ramming the gear-stick viciously into first.

She'd been driving for several miles before her sense of humour began to re-emerge, and a rueful little smile touched her lips. She'd come to the Lake District in part at least to rest and revitalise her jaded soul. Meeting up with a chauvinistic caveman just a few miles over the county boundary and succumbing to his Neanderthal but overwhelming charm in a lay-by definitely wasn't what any doctor would have ordered. By any standards it had not been an auspicious start.

CHAPTER TWO

THE hotel was relatively small but with a quiet, understated elegance that instantly had a soothing effect on Clancy's jangled nerves. Definitely not the sort of place where she was likely to encounter any more latter-day highwaymen, she reflected as she signed the register, refusing to acknowledge the tiny shadow of regret that accompanied the thought.

'Do you know how long you'll be staying with us, Miss Hall?' the receptionist queried.

Clancy shook her head. 'Not yet. Two or three days, I should think. Can I let you know later?'

The young woman smiled. 'Of course. At this time of year we're generally fairly quiet, so there shouldn't be a problem. Now, shall I call the porter to carry your luggage upstairs to your room?'

Clancy smiled. 'No, I only have this one bag. I can manage.'

Travelling light was something she'd become very accustomed to in the past few years since becoming part of the small, independent television company she'd helped to found. It had been a tough time in many ways, she thought ruefully, closing the bedroom door behind her with a satisfied sigh as she eyed the big old-fashioned bed—surely in that she'd be able to find the rest that had been eluding her so drastically recently? First, though, she'd take that long, hot bath she'd been promising herself, then order a meal to be sent up, since she didn't feel like facing anyone tonight. Opportunities to be so shamelessly self-indulgent were rare indeed these days.

Dan's concerned voice came filtering back as she unpacked and she smiled, remembering the faintly anxious look in his warm brown eyes.

'You really need a break,' he'd said bluntly. 'You've been working far too hard.'

'No more than you or any of the others,' she'd countered.

He shook his head. 'Look, Clance, I know you better than anyone else in the world, and I know how hard that last trip was on you. It wore you out—emotionally as well as physically.'

She looked away, feeling the sting of tears that seemed to come all too readily these days.

'I'm a researcher. I'm supposed to be able to deal with things objectively.'

'You're also a human being,' he retorted sharply. 'And one with more heart and soul than most.' His lips tightened. 'Since you came back you've been as taut as a violin string—and that's at least partly because you won't allow yourself to admit how deeply you were affected. Why, Clancy? Are you afraid people will think the less of your professional capabilities?'

She'd managed to fob him off with excuses then, but she'd known it would be at best only a temporary reprieve. Sure enough, he'd waited just a couple of days before tackling her again. This time, though, it was to give her a new assignment.

'You want to do a documentary on the Lake District? Why?'

'Why not?' His answering expression was utterly bland. 'It's an incredibly beautiful place.'

'Granted—I can see you'd get a lot of pretty pictures—but it's not exactly the sort of thing we usually get involved in.'

Dan shrugged. 'We've built the company's reputation on our willingness to boldly go where other television crews would really rather not venture, thank you very much. But there's no reason why we can't start to become a bit more versatile now. Branch out a bit.'

She couldn't help but smile. He made it sound as though they'd been through a *Boys' Own* adventure, but she'd been with Dan and the rest of the crew as they risked their lives in countries torn by civil war and strife. He thrived on danger, relished new challenges. She could barely believe he'd want to turn his attention to something that seemed on the surface at least to be little more than a travelogue. Unless... She raised suspicious eyes to his.

'Are you doing this because of me?'

'I haven't the faintest idea what you mean.' But his eyes flickered away from hers and she frowned. She'd always been able to read her twin brother like a book.

'Don't give me that! This is Clancy, remember? Have you been cooking something up with Mum and Dad?'

When he grinned sheepishly, she knew she'd hit pay-dirt and her frown deepened to a scowl.

'Forget it. You're not packing me off to the Lakes like some invalid in need of a rest-cure.'

'It's not like that, Clance,' Dan remonstrated. 'They're concerned about you. Come to that, so am I. You're as thin as a rake, you hardly eat enough to keep a sparrow alive and you've lost your old sparkle.' With brotherly affection he took her hands, his voice coaxing as he continued, 'That last trip really got to you, didn't it? You can tell me, for Pete's sake!'

She took a deep breath, feeling all over again the agonies she'd suffered on seeing the desolate sun-baked landscape and the famine-ravaged people of Sudan. They were pictures which would never leave her, pictures that still haunted her dreams by night and tainted every mouthful of food she ate with bitter guilt.

'I don't want to talk about it,' she said stubbornly.

Dan banged his fist on the table in frustration. 'Dammit, Clancy, that's exactly the problem! You'll never get it out of your system till you do talk about it. Can't you see that?'

She could see it perfectly well—but in a very real sense she didn't want to 'get it out of her system'. The things she'd seen had made her deeply ashamed. Before the trip she'd have said she came from a very ordinary background, the type of home where special treats such as holidays had to be scrimped and saved for. But her life had been positively luxurious in comparison to those poor suffering people. Doing the documentary had helped them a little—had triggered a staggering number of people into acts of over-whelming generosity. But though she'd been moved to tears by their giving, Clancy knew it could do no more than scratch at the very surface of what was a monumental problem.

She climbed wearily into the bath, feeling some of the deep-seated tension in her bones ease with the warmth of the water as she closed her eyes. At least she'd managed to talk Dan out of his nonsensical idea for doing a documentary on the Lake District—even though it had taken all the persuasive tactics she could muster. Now her brief was to do background research for an in-depth look at mountain rescue teams—the valiant men and women who regularly risked their lives to save others, and all on a purely voluntary basis.

Unconsciously swishing her fingers through the foaming water, she found herself wondering about the man she was due to meet the following morning. She'd spent several days doing what research she could into the various teams which covered the beautiful but sometimes treacherous Lake District territory, before choosing the one she wanted to feature in the programme. She still wasn't entirely sure what had prompted her choice. The team was a long-established one, with an excellent record of bringing stranded and often seriously injured climbers safely down from the hills, but that was equally true of the other groups.

Her eyes narrowed thoughtfully as she remembered the letter she'd received from the group leader. Handwritten, it had been brief and to the point and far less friendly than some of the others she'd received in reply to the letters she'd sent outlining her intentions. And yet—something about that distinctive heavy black scrawl had intrigued her. Luke MacLennan. She turned the name over in her mind, trying to picture the man behind it. It was a strong, uncompromising name, and from what she'd been able to glean so far a name that fitted his personality. From talking to local journalists she knew Luke MacLennan had been leading the team for the past ten years, and that he also owned and ran a company specialising in adventure courses. It was clear he was all but idolised in the area—and perhaps a little feared too.

'Not a good man to cross.'

'Doesn't suffer fools gladly.'

'Doesn't suffer fools at all!'

'A great man—but not an easy one to get close to.'

Feeling the water begin to grow uncomfortably cool, Clancy gave a dismissive little shrug. It wasn't her job to get close to Luke MacLennan—or anyone else for that matter. She simply had to find out as many details about him and the other team members as possible, and go on a couple of recce trips into the hills. The rest was up to Dan and the crew.

Yawning widely, she climbed out of the bath and wrapped herself in a warm towelling robe. Unthinkingly she paused to glance at her own reflection in the mirror, then gave a rueful little grimace. As much as she hated to admit it, the blasted man in the lay-by had been right. She did look a wreck—her skin pale and stretched over her cheekbones, and heavy shadows beneath her huge hazel eyes.

Then she scowled. Why on earth had she thought about him again, for goodness' sake? His opinion meant nothing—less than nothing. He was nothing more than a king-size hunk of sheer undiluted ar-

rogant machismo. Glowering back at herself as though
she was looking into his face, she gave a satisfied nod.
There—that had him neatly wrapped up and labelled.
And summarily dismissed from her thoughts. Which,
if she had anything to do with it, was exactly where
he would stay.

Rather to her surprise, Clancy slept well that night,
free for once of the dreams that had been plaguing
her ever since her return to Britain. Waking to the
grey light of an early winter morning, she turned over
in bed, stretching luxuriously before throwing back
the covers. Knowing she had time to spare, she
lingered over showering, enjoying the gentle warmth
of the water as it cascaded over her skin. Not that
she'd ever be able to take things like showers for
granted again, she reminded herself as she briskly
rubbed down with a soft towel—in that dry, barren
land so very far away, water had been more precious
than gold. Even now it was impossible to watch that
invaluable commodity simply trickling away down the
drain without a severe pang.

   Unconsciously she sighed as she reached for the
trousers and sweater she'd laid out the night before,
wondering if she'd ever be able to feel frivolous or
light-hearted again. Then she frowned, annoyed with
herself. How could she even want to be frivolous now
that she'd seen for herself the agonies other people
went through in order simply to survive? Still—there
was a part of her that missed the lost joyous part of
her soul, the part that had rejoiced to see a beautiful
sunset, or to read a moving poem.

Shrugging off the thought, she dressed swiftly then headed downstairs to the hotel dining-room for breakfast. Despite her good intentions, she hadn't eaten the previous evening, and now she was conscious of a niggling little ache of hunger. Her appetite vanished completely, however, when the waitress appeared, bearing a plate piled high with sausage, bacon, egg, fried bread and mushrooms.

'I'm terribly sorry,' Clancy said apologetically. 'I can't possibly eat all that.'

'Nonsense.' The motherly-looking woman grinned back unperturbed. 'The weather's turned cold today— you need something warm and nourishing.' She eyed Clancy critically. 'Besides which you look as if you could do with a decent meal.'

Clancy couldn't help but smile, unoffended by her frankness. But she shook her head adamantly.

'I only ever take toast and coffee in the morning. Perhaps I should have told Reception that last night when I booked in.'

The waitress pursed her lips. 'That's not enough to keep the kitchen cat alive.'

'Really, it's all I want.'

They stared at each other in a silent battle of wills. It was clear the older woman was caught between genuine concern and the need to accede to the wishes of a guest. In the end the waitress in her won the day, though she made her disapproval clear with a shake of her head.

'Very well, miss,' she said. 'But I'll bring the same to you tomorrow morning. If our good clean Lake

District air doesn't give you a proper appetite, my name's not Margery Wilson.'

Clancy was still smiling a touch wryly half an hour later as she drove out of the hotel car park on her way to meet Luke MacLennan. Who'd have thought she'd meet such a termagant in a hotel dining-room? Aware that she was still under the redoubtable Margery's eagle eye, she'd forced herself to eat two pieces of toast, and to take milk in the coffee she normally drank black. It had been disconcerting to find such concern coming from a total stranger, an invasion of the privacy she set such store by. Still, she couldn't deny it had been strangely warming, too, bolstering her to face the meeting ahead.

That thought puzzled her as she reached her destination. Why should she need bolstering? She was only going to meet a man who'd agreed to take part in a programme—it wasn't anything she hadn't done dozens of times before. And yet—she knew a faint tremor of apprehension as she gave her name to a young female receptionist and took the seat pointed out to her. Unsettled by a surge of unaccustomed nervousness, she took a small mirror from her bag to check her make-up, irritated to see that she'd unconsciously licked off all the lipstick she'd applied so painstakingly just a short while before.

'Miss Hall? Mr MacLennan will see you now.'

Clancy wondered at the faint but unmistakable trace of amusement in the young woman's voice as she followed her into the office. Then she stopped dead in her tracks as a man rose from his chair. Her expression of amazement was mirrored by his.

'You're Luke MacLennan?'

'And you're C. J. Hall?'

Behind them the door closed discreetly. It was he who recovered his composure first, waving a hand towards a chair at the opposite side of the desk.

'I expected C. J. Hall to be male,' he said abruptly.

Uncomfortably aware that her heart for some inexplicable reason was racing twenty to the dozen, Clancy subsided into the chair.

'And I expected Luke MacLennan to be a mountain rescue team leader, not a hijacker of innocent females,' she retorted. 'So we're quits.'

'Your letter didn't make it clear you were female,' he continued, ignoring her words.

'Why should it have?' Sensing a spot of chauvinism about to be unleashed, Clancy glared back at him darkly. 'Surely it makes no difference. Or does it?'

He steepled his fingers beneath his chin, his smoke-grey eyes regarding her assessingly. 'You seem to think it does.'

'I do?' Her eyes widened in astonishment. 'That's utterly ridiculous.'

'Is it?' There was no change in his expression. 'Then why sign your letters in such a deliberately anonymous way? If you really do believe it makes no difference, then why not use the customary Miss, or Ms?' He glanced downwards at her unadorned left hand. 'Or Mrs?'

'I'm not married,' she spat back, uncharacteristically rattled. 'But even if I were I don't see why I should have to advertise that fact to the world.'

'Why not?' There was a glint of amusement in his dark eyes that only served to annoy her all the more. 'Most women seem to take pride in being married.'

'For one thing, I am not "most women",' she shot back. 'I don't believe in running with the herd.'

Now his amusement was blatant, curving his lips into a mocking smile. 'Rather a harsh dismissal of your entire sex,' he said mildly. 'What's the other thing?'

Now he had her completely confused. 'Other thing?'

'You said "for one thing"—I assumed the statement would have a second half.'

She bit her lip, conscious of a growing anger bubbling up within. This blasted man was playing with her—dangling her on a string as if she were a puppet. If the programme weren't so important, she'd take enormous delight in telling him to take a long walk off a very short pier.

'For another thing, men aren't expected to identify their status in the same manner,' she said, her words curt and clipped. 'You, for example, are simply Mr Luke MacLennan—that gives no clue whatsoever as to whether...'

'As to whether or not I'm married,' he completed the sentence for her, then leaned back in his seat, regarding her steadily. 'If you wish to know, you only have to ask.'

'I have no desire whatsoever to know!' She all but yelled the words back at him, growing frustration thwarting her desire to keep her temper in check. 'I couldn't care less if you were married and had fourteen children. It's the principle of the thing I'm talking about.'

'So, when you fell into my arms in that lay-by, you never even stopped to consider my wife and fourteen children?' He shook his head reprovingly. 'How very immoral of you, C. J. Hall.'

He was laughing at her and she knew it, but her own sense of humour seemed to have vanished into thin air. She clenched her hands into fists, mentally counting to ten.

'Look,' she managed at last, 'this is utterly ridiculous. As you are perfectly aware, I did not fall into your arms. Furthermore, had I realised your identity there and then I'd have jumped into the car and headed straight back to London. However, I'm here and I intend to carry out the job I've been assigned to do. I'd rather do it with your co-operation. So, shall we start all over again?'

Before he had time to answer, she rushed on, 'Good morning, Mr MacLennan, my name is Clancy Hall and I am the researcher who wrote to you with a view to doing a documentary programme on mountain rescue teams. I'm here today to find out when you'll be free to take me on a recce into the hills. When you've done that, I shall return to London, report my findings to the production crew and leave them to it. Now—over to you.'

'Just like that?' One dark eyebrow quirked upwards. 'You expect to simply head off into the hills for a jolly little jaunt, just like that?'

'Not a "jolly little jaunt", no,' she returned exasperatedly. 'I appreciate that the work you do up there is of a serious nature, and, believe me, I'm prepared to treat the trip in a serious manner.'

He gave a single nod. 'I'm delighted to hear it. Then you'll be quite happy to undergo a programme of preparation beforehand.'

She was about to accede unthinkingly to what seemed on the face of it a perfectly reasonable request when a niggle of doubt got in the way. She hardly knew this man from Adam, yet something inside was warning her to look before she leapt, and she'd learned from past experience it was never wise to ignore intuition. Her eyes narrowed suspiciously.

'What sort of programme, exactly?'

'One which I'll personally devise. To establish whether you're fit enough to venture into the hills.'

For once in her life she was rendered speechless as her eyes widened in astonishment at the sheer gall of the man. He was questioning her fitness? Granted, he had no way of knowing the gruelling conditions she'd faced in Sudan, conditions she could never have hoped to cope with had she been less than fit, but his insinuation was nothing less than insulting.

'What exactly are you suggesting, Mr MacLennan?'

If he heard the ice in her voice he gave no sign of it, his own expression remaining neutral. 'I wasn't aware I was suggesting anything, Miss Hall,' he returned evenly. 'I was stating a condition. Since I apparently didn't make myself sufficiently clear, I'll spell it out for you a second time. I will take you on your recce trip when and only when I'm satisfied that you're capable of it.'

'But this is ridiculous!' The words burst from her before she could stop them. 'People go into the hills all the time. None of them has to submit to a test first.'

'Which is partly why rescue teams exist,' he said calmly, unmoved by her anger. He held up one hand to forestall her next words. 'I assume you're about to point out that even the fittest of climbers can suffer accidents, and that's quite correct.' His dark eyes hardened to slate as they seemed to bore into her. 'However, Miss Hall, I regret to say there are also those misguided enough to treat the mountains as a game. If I'm to be involved in your documentary, I intend to ensure you do not fall into that category.'

She bit her lip, fuming silently, her anger made all the more intense by an irritating little inner voice which would keep telling her he was right. It was as much to silence that voice as to hit back at him that she tilted her chin scornfully in his direction.

'I take it you feel you have some sort of divine right over the hills, Mr MacLennan? You would prefer that every walker and climber had to come and seek your gracious permission before setting foot on your precious territory?'

If she'd hoped to annoy him, she'd clearly failed.

'On the contrary, Miss Hall. The hills and fells are open to everyone and I wouldn't have it any other way. They've inspired some of our greatest minds, and they've brought balm to many wounded souls.' He paused, eyeing her thoughtfully, and the breath seemed to lodge in her throat. Was he suggesting she was a wounded soul? Before she could form any kind of a protest, he began speaking again.

'However, they can never be taken for granted, or treated frivolously. Men—and women for that matter—have died because they didn't treat them with the respect they both deserve and demand.'

She dropped her eyes, his stark words making her ruefully aware she'd been childishly petulant—and equally aware he had her completely at a disadvantage. He'd seen people die in the hills—he hadn't said as much, but for a moment as he'd spoken she'd seen the pain of memories that wouldn't fade in his dark eyes. To continue with her protests now would be unthinkable. Unconsciously she gave a faint surrendering sigh, then raised her eyes to his.

'Very well, Mr MacLennan,' she said with quiet resignation. 'I accept your conditions. I'll undergo some sort of fitness test if that's what it takes to convince you I'm not likely to keel over from exhaustion after the first five minutes of walking. Will that satisfy you?'

CHAPTER THREE

FOR the most fleeting of seconds there seemed to be a flicker of sympathy in Luke's smoky grey eyes, and Clancy wondered at it even as it made her bridle inwardly. She didn't need this man's sympathy—or anyone else's, come to that. And why on earth should he think she did?

Hostility tautened her own features as she gazed back at him across the wide expanse of desk, the lengthening silence making her uncomfortable.

'I asked you a question,' she said shortly.

He gave a barely perceptible nod. 'And I'm considering my response.'

She frowned uncomprehendingly. 'What is there to consider? I've agreed to your conditions. Surely that's all there is to it.'

'Not quite.' He leaned forward in his chair, resting his elbows on the desk as he eyed her openly, his eyes raking her face as though searching for answers. She wanted to turn away, gripped by a strange and inexplicable desire to flee from his all too perceptive gaze, managing only with a supreme effort of will to hold her head high.

'How long do you intend to stay in the Lake District?'

The question caught her by surprise. 'I hadn't decided exactly,' she hedged. 'As long as it takes. A couple of days—three or four at the most.'

He shook his head decisively. 'That won't do. If you want to do this properly, you'll need to reckon on weeks rather than days.'

'Weeks?' Her hazel eyes widened to their fullest extent. 'That's impossible. I can't possibly...'

'Waste that much time?' Scorn was evident in the twist of his mouth. 'Is that what you were about to say?'

She flinched, horribly aware that he'd guessed accurately. 'Perhaps I was, but not in the way you think. I have other assignments in hand—other work I'm committed to doing.' Which was a lie, since Dan had made it clear she could take as much time as she needed to set up the mountain rescue shoot. That had annoyed her at the time—she knew perfectly well that their small, independent company could ill afford the luxury of having researchers out in the field for any longer than was strictly necessary.

'Forget those other assignments,' Luke said abruptly. 'Or else forget this one. I won't allow my team to participate in anything half-baked.'

She scowled at that, angered by the slur on her professional abilities. 'My research is never half-baked,' she retorted. 'I pride myself on doing a thorough job, no matter what the subject.'

Rather to her surprise he smiled and something deep within her stirred restlessly, something which had been slumbering undisturbed for a long, long time.

'I'm delighted to hear it,' he said. 'So that's settled, then.'

'Not quite,' she shot back, reluctant to hand control of the situation over to him quite so readily. 'You haven't yet explained why I need to stay so long. And, frankly, if I'm to convince my partner I need so much time, I'll need more than just your say-so.' Which was also a blatant lie, but he didn't need to know that.

Annoyance flickered briefly over his features and she mentally notched up one point to the home team. He clearly wasn't accustomed to having his commands questioned. Well, if she did go along with this scheme of his, he'd better start getting used to it and fast. Clancy J. Hall wasn't anyone's submissive poodle, no matter how gorgeous he was.

'You need the time to build up your strength,' he said.

She shook her head dismissively. 'I'm strong already.'

'You think so?'

Unconsciously she sat up straighter in the chair, jutting her chin defiantly. 'Don't be fooled by appearances, Mr MacLennan. I may be slight in stature, but I'm more than capable of a considerable amount of physical exertion.'

Something akin to amusement glittered in the depths of his eyes. 'So I gathered in the lay-by yesterday,' he murmured.

A mixture of shock and embarrassment flooded her pale cheeks with hot colour and she gasped aloud. 'How dare you? That's not what I meant and you know it. In fact——' she sent him her haughtiest look

'—if I'm to agree to your conditions, I'd like to stipulate one of my own.'

'Which is?' He raised one querying eyebrow.

'Which is that we both forget that highly regrettable incident ever took place, and that we never refer to it again.'

He considered that for a moment, his eyes never leaving her face. 'Why should that matter to you so much?' he said at last, and she wasn't sure whether he was speaking to himself or to her.

'Why? Because such a thing should never have happened in the first place, that's why. And because it will be hard enough to build any kind of working relationship after such a tawdry beginning without having it constantly referred to.' She sat back, folding her arms in an unconsciously defensive gesture.

'Tawdry?' He seemed to examine the word. 'A rather revealing choice of adjective, Miss Hall. Why should genuine spontaneous passion be dismissed as tawdry?'

'"Spontaneous passion"?' She echoed his words incredulously. 'Is that how you remember it?' She shook her head, barely able to believe what she'd just heard. 'I'm afraid I put a rather different interpretation on it, Mr MacLennan.'

'Which is what, exactly?' A smile played about the corners of his mouth and she was furious to find herself on the verge of thawing to him—all because of a stupid smile! Get a grip, girl, she admonished herself silently. Don't allow him to manipulate you like this.

'Which is that you simply assumed—took it for granted—that I'd be perfectly happy to succumb to your charms. Maybe you even thought I'd be flattered by your attentions. But you were wrong. Totally wrong.' Almost as if she could feel the scorching touch of his mouth on hers all over again, she licked her lips unthinkingly. His eyes darkened at the gesture.

'You're a very accomplished liar, Miss Hall,' he said, and she shivered at the coldness in his tone. 'Perhaps even to yourself—because when I kissed the woman I held in my arms yesterday she gave back every bit as much as she was receiving.'

'How dare you?' Scandalised, Clancy leapt to her feet, her eyes blazing.

'How dare I?' He was openly mocking now, his ease as he sat back in the chair a total contrast to her own highly strung state. 'Perhaps because I'm not afraid to acknowledge the needs of my own body.'

'And I suppose you always give it exactly what it wants,' she spat back scathingly, too far gone in anger now to really know what she was saying.

He gave a slight shrug. 'Not always. But at least I don't deny the feelings.'

'And you think I do?'

'I *know* you do.' The emphasis on the second word was faint but definite. 'But that's going to have to change. Over the next few weeks you'll have to learn all over again how to listen to the things your body is telling you. You'll have to recognise the signs of hunger, or tiredness, or strain, and you'll have to know how to cope with them.'

'Don't be ridiculous, Mr MacLennan.' Her lips twisted scornfully. 'I'm a human being, not a robot. I already know how to recognise those things.'

'Are you so sure of that?' He spoke softly, yet the challenge in his voice was unmistakable. 'In this modern and so-called civilised world of ours we've programmed ourselves—we eat and sleep when the clock on the wall tells us it's time to do so. We may miss the odd meal here and there, or stay up later than usual on party nights, but nevertheless for the most part we act according to schedules laid down by the society we live in.'

Unthinkingly Clancy subsided back into the chair she'd leapt from just a few moments before. Almost despite herself she was intrigued, forced to recognise the truth in his words. Her own professional life was far from the standard nine-to-five existence experienced by so many, yet the kind of deadlines it imposed were uncompromising, creating in their own way a framework even more rigid than the one he'd described.

The only time the framework had really been tested had been in Sudan, she remembered now, strangely disturbed by the realisation that this was the first time in hours she'd given a thought to that bare, parched land. It had never been out of her mind for longer than a few seconds since she'd been home—until today.

'What is it?' he said sharply. 'What are you thinking?'

Her eyes, strangely unfocused, lifted to his face. 'Thinking?' she echoed uncertainly.

'A shadow passed over your face,' he said. 'Un-happy thoughts, perhaps?'

She smiled mirthlessly, wondering fleetingly just how he'd react if she did tell him exactly what she'd been thinking. Dan had been begging her to share her troubled thoughts with someone—to unburden herself of the load she'd been carrying. She'd found it im-possible, even with close friends—even with Dan and the other crew members who'd been there too. She could never tell this man of the anguish she'd suf-fered, even though ironically there was a part of her that suddenly found itself longing to let go.

She shivered, remembering the feel of those strong arms around her. As much as she might deny it to him, she could never deny it to herself. She had felt passion for this stranger, but there had been some-thing else too, something she'd rejected even as she hungered for it. In his embrace she'd felt strangely secure and protected. Perhaps that was under-standable given his role as mountain rescue team leader—he was accustomed to providing security and succour for lost souls. Somehow she must have sensed that, even as she struggled.

Confused by the turn of her own thoughts, she forced herself to give a light little laugh. 'I'm sorry, I was wool-gathering,' she said dismissively. 'Where were we?'

His eyes narrowed and for a moment she thought he'd refuse to be so easily diverted. But at last he nodded.

'Very well, Miss Hall,' he said evenly. 'If you're determined to close your mind to me, so be it. For

now.' He began describing the programme he had in
mind for her, but she found it hard to concentrate,
her thoughts still focused on that last, telling remark.
What had he meant by 'for now'? He hadn't sounded
overtly threatening, yet there had been an underlying
challenge in his words. What was she letting herself
in for? Then she gave herself a mental shake. She
could handle Luke MacLennan. He might be big and
powerful, and he might pack more sensuality than any
other man she'd ever met, but she could cope with
that. She hoped.

Clancy made her way along the street, glancing in shop
windows as she passed, unconsciously grimacing as
she realised most of them were blatantly and uncom-
promisingly aimed at the tourist trade. Well, what else
could she expect? she reasoned wearily. The Lake
District was very much a tourist area, a veritable
honeypot, drawing visitors in their thousands. She
could only thank heaven she was here off-season, for
doubtless the narrow streets of this small town would
be jam-packed in the summer months. Right now what
her jaded soul craved was solitude—peace and quiet
and a chance to get back in touch with her own inner
self.

   Glancing up at the place-name on the wall, she
turned down a side-street, her eyes searching out the
shop signs as she looked for one in particular. In her
hand she was clutching a list of all the things Luke
MacLennan insisted she'd need over the next few
weeks. A fresh wave of irritation washed over her as
she glanced at the crumpled paper—just who did he

think he was, ordering her to buy all these items? And who did he think *she* was—a millionaire?

'An ice-axe?' She'd looked at him in blank disbelief after running her eye swiftly over the things he'd noted down. 'You want me to buy an ice-axe? Why?'

'Because it's an essential piece of equipment on the hills in the winter,' he'd returned patiently.

'Couldn't I simply borrow one from someone on the team?'

He frowned darkly. 'And what would he or she use in its place?' He shook his head abruptly. 'No. You buy your own gear.'

'And what am I supposed to do with it when I'm finished here?' she remonstrated. 'Strangely enough, I haven't often found much need for an ice-axe in London.'

He smiled, and, much as she tried to prevent it, her heart turned right over at the sight. He truly was a stunningly good-looking man.

'When you're finished with the gear, you can donate it to the team,' he said. 'We always need new equipment.'

'So that's what this is all about!' Indignation flooded her veins as she glowered darkly back at him. 'You people are all the same—you see the words ''television programme'' and they instantly turn into dollar signs before your very eyes. You think you'll take us for every penny you can screw out of us, because you assume we must be rolling in money. Well, let me put you straight on that, Mr MacLennan. Ours is a small, independent company—we have to work, and work damn hard, to complete every production we ever undertake, and we do it on a veritable shoe-string. We are not, I repeat *not*, the fat cats of the industry.'

His dark eyes narrowed dangerously and she felt a twinge of fear. Luke MacLennan wasn't a man to be trifled with—she'd realised that within seconds of their first meeting. She'd only been speaking the truth, but had she pushed him too far?

'I suggest you don't talk to me or to any of my team members about ''shoestring'' budgets, Miss Hall,' he said quietly but with a wealth of meaning. 'Unless you're prepared to eat humble pie, that is.'

'I realise your team is self-financing,' she cut in, making a valiant bid to claw back the ground she could practically see crumbling beneath her feet. 'But surely...?'

'Surely what?' His eyes were positively glacial now and she was hard pressed to suppress a shiver, pierced through by the shards of ice in his voice. 'Surely we can afford to buy our own equipment? Surely we're not reduced to begging from television companies? It so happens that our entire operation is financed through the generosity of the public—through donations and fund-raising ventures. As you should know if you've done your research, we get no government funding. Yet we are in the job of saving lives, Miss Hall, and we do it well.'

She looked away then, ashamed of her own pettiness. She'd spoken impetuously and thoughtlessly and now she regretted it—partly because she knew she'd been unfair, but also because of the scorn in his eyes which she knew was deserved.

'I'm sorry,' she said quietly. 'I spoke out of turn. I'm sure my company will be happy to foot the bill for the equipment.' If she was wrong, if Dan balked at adding more to the budget, then she'd simply have to dip into her own savings, though they were far from substantial. Going into partnership with Dan had taken almost every penny she possessed, and, even though business was good now, still it would be a long time before she could hope to recoup what she'd spent.

In the event the shop he'd sent her to turned out to have a second-hand department and she was able to pick up almost everything on his list there. He'd doubtless known that would be the case, she reflected ruefully as she arranged for all the gear to be sent to her hotel, and it made her outburst all the more regrettable.

She walked slowly back to the hotel, weighed down by an uncomfortable cloud of depression. She had to spend the next few weeks in his company, a prospect which was presumably as uninviting to him as it was to her. It didn't help her state of mind to know that in different circumstances she'd have been attracted to him. Even now, after two meetings which could only be described as disastrous, she was worryingly aware that she was far from immune to him.

The telephone was ringing as she entered the bedroom, but she let it ring for a moment, kicking off her shoes and flinging herself down on the big double bed before resignedly reaching for the receiver.

'Hello, Dan.'

'Hello, yourself.'

He wasn't in the least surprised that she'd known it was him on the other end of the line. A lifetime of being as closely bonded as only twins could be meant they always knew what the other one was feeling, even from a distance of many miles. He'd probably been picking up on her unsettled vibrations all day long, she realised with a wry smile—and no doubt had been consumed with curiosity to know just what had caused them.

'So how are things up there in the beautiful Lake District?' he asked now.

'Terrific. Couldn't be better.'

'Liar.'

She sighed audibly. It would be nice just once to be able to fool him. 'Honestly, Dan,' she said without much hope. 'Everything's just great. Hunky-dory, in fact.'

'Liar.'

'For goodness' sake! What does it take to convince you?'

'Well, the truth would make a good start.' His voice grew more gentle. 'Come on, Clance, this is Dan you're talking to, remember? What's the problem? And don't bother even trying to tell me there isn't one, because I know perfectly well there is.'

Clancy closed her eyes and counted silently to ten. Just once in a while the perceptiveness of her twin was more of a burden than a blessing, and this was one of those times.

'OK,' she said at last. 'The problem is Luke MacLennan.'

'Ah.' Somehow he managed to convey a wealth of understanding in the single syllable. 'The hero of the mountains is a royal pain, is he? I know the type— thermal socks and a full beard and a voice loud enough to start avalanches all on its own. And,' he went on, warming to his theme, 'I bet he strides around as though he were wearing seven-league boots, muttering darkly about the destructiveness of man and the foolishness of women.'

Almost despite herself Clancy began to laugh. Wouldn't it be wonderful if Luke MacLennan really were as Dan had described? A man like that she could handle before breakfast. 'Not quite,' she said. 'He's more the steely and determined type—a bit enigmatic, but dynamic with it.'

'Is that a fact?' Dan's voice grew thoughtful. 'Steely, determined, enigmatic *and* dynamic? Is he good-looking as well?'

'Absolutely gorgeous.' Clancy bit her lip, horrified at her own lack of forethought.

'Hellfire!' Even along an anonymous phone wire, Dan sounded awestruck. 'Sounds as if you're in big trouble, girl.'

'I am? Why?'

'Because he sounds just the type you've been waiting for all these years.'

'Don't be ridiculous.' Thoroughly nettled, Clancy sat bolt upright on the bed, scowling darkly as though he could see her.

'You may mock, my sweet one, but I know the kind of man it'll take to sweep you off your firmly planted little feet. And Luke MacLennan fits the bill. To a "T".'

'I wouldn't have him if he were the last man on earth,' she returned firmly. 'Furthermore, I most certainly have not been waiting for anyone. I'm just like you—perfectly happy to fly solo.'

'Hmm.' He was clearly unconvinced. 'No one should fly solo forever, not even me and definitely not you. You need a soul-mate.'

'And it seems I already have one in you, whether I want it or not,' she returned drily. 'So will you kindly shut up about it before I slam this phone down?'

He chuckled delightedly. 'Slam away, princess—you know perfectly well that will only sever the *artificial* connection between us—it won't do anything to stop me picking up on the way you're feeling, and, believe you me, right now it's coming through loud and clear.'

Clancy sighed heavily. She should be well accustomed to Dan's teasing by now—heaven knew she'd been enduring it for twenty-seven years, ever since they'd been in the cradle together. She knew too that it was well-intentioned. He would never hurt her for the world, and woe betide anyone else who even thought of it. If Dan truly believed Luke was giving her a hard time, he'd be on the next train to Cumbria, full of wrath and indignation, ready to sort him out, even though Luke was at least twice his size. It was a comforting thought but she pushed it resolutely out of her mind. As far as Luke was concerned, she was on her own.

'So come on, Clancy, spell it out. What's the problem?'

She shook her head determinedly. 'Nothing I can't handle. But it looks as though I'll have to stay here longer than we originally planned.'

'Oh? Why?'

'Because Luke seems to think I'm not fit enough to tackle his precious mountains yet.' There was a wealth of disgust in her voice, but if she'd hoped her twin would be equally annoyed she was in for a disappointment.

'He's right. You're not.'

'What? You're just as bad as he is, you...you... Judas!'

'Seriously, Clance, this Luke MacLennan sounds like a good man. And he knows his job. Frankly I'm a lot happier about you being up there all alone now I know he's there to keep an eye on you.'

'What is this?' If he could but have seen, her eyes were shooting sparks of anger, her cheeks beginning to flame with anger. 'May I remind you you're my twin, and my younger twin at that, not my keeper? How dare you concern yourself about where I am and what I'm doing there?'

'Because I love you, that's why.' His quiet words cut into her tirade. 'And I worry about you. I know perfectly well that goes against your independent grain, but there it is. I've been concerned about you ever since we got back from Sudan. If this MacLennan guy thinks he can whip you back into some sort of shape, then good luck to him. He has my blessing.'

Clancy lay back against the pillows, closing her eyes in utter weary resignation. It was a male conspiracy—

it had to be. Had Dan and Luke somehow cooked
this up between them?

'Have you ever met Luke?' she asked suspiciously.

'Nope. But I'm looking forward to it. He sounds
like quite a guy.'

'Well, just make sure you and the rest of the crew
are fit,' she returned sarkily. 'Otherwise he won't have
anything to do with you.'

Dan's rich chuckle reverberated along the line and
she couldn't help but smile in response. A nuisance
he might be, but she wouldn't change him for the
world. They chatted for a few minutes longer, then
she hung up, feeling better for having talked to him.

'"Quite a guy",' she muttered softly as she replaced the receiver. That was one way to describe
Luke—one way among many, and even on short acquaintance she could think of several others, not all
of them complimentary. Then she frowned, realising
she'd been using his Christian name in her mind. That
would have to stop. The only way she could hope to
cope was to keep him safely at arm's length, and the
best way to do that was to keep things strictly formal.

Not that he was likely to want it any other way, she
reminded herself bleakly. After that first heated
meeting, he hadn't shown the remotest sign of being
attracted to her—hell, he didn't even seem to like her
very much! Well, that was just fine by her, because
she didn't like him much either.

Still—her features grew pensive as she pictured his
face in her mind's eye—she couldn't help but wonder
what it would be like to see warmth in those smoky
grey eyes, feel tenderness from those incredibly sensual

lips, hear soft words of love whispered in that husky masculine voice.

She sat up abruptly, her eyes wide with horror. Love? Where in the name of all things wonderful had that word suddenly appeared from? She'd admit to feeling a physical attraction for him—lust, if she wanted to be downright basic about it—but that was all. She shook her head disgustedly as if that would help banish the wayward thoughts. If Dan were to pick up on those, he'd be back on the phone in seconds, demanding to know everything, and she couldn't bear the teasing if he was ever to find out about that ridiculous episode in the lay-by.

She slid off the bed, wandering aimlessly about the room till she stopped before the full-length mirror on the wall, her attention caught by her own reflection. What was it about her that had convinced both Dan and Luke she was less than a hundred per cent fit?

Her eyes ran critically over her own image—OK, so she was slender to the point of being thin, but she always had been. Beneath the faded remains of the tan she'd developed abroad she was pale, but that too was nothing unusual. Anyway, fair skin normally went hand in hand with her type of auburn hair.

Then she bit her lip as she looked deep into her own hazel eyes. They were the give-away. Once clear, bright and merry, now they looked shadowed and haunted—the eyes of a woman who'd looked into hell. Had she changed forever? She scowled ferociously at her own reflection, unconsciously straightening her shoulders. No way—the Halls were made of sterner stuff and she'd prove it, no matter what it took. Furthermore, she'd do it despite Luke MacLennan, not because of him.

She gave a resolute little nod, strangely warmed by a new feeling of strength. She might have got off on the wrong foot with the man of the mountains—but he had yet to discover just what Clancy J. Hall was capable of.

CHAPTER FOUR

'MISS HALL? Good morning—I hope I haven't disturbed you. Mr MacLennan is waiting downstairs for you.'

Clancy's heart plummeted to the soles of her feet with the receptionist's words. He was in the hotel already? She'd hoped to have a little time to psych herself up for the day ahead, but it seemed she wasn't even to be allowed to breakfast in peace.

'Please tell him I'll join him in a few moments,' she responded tonelessly, then replaced the receiver with a disgruntled sigh. Blasted man! Didn't he have anything better to do with his time than harass her? He'd probably expected to find her still in bed, she thought with a scowl—thank goodness she was up and dressed, or he'd doubtless have grabbed yet another opportunity to criticise her.

She made her way slowly downstairs, vainly trying to put off the moment of seeing him again. And yet— when she spotted his tall, imposing figure in the foyer and watched him swivel round to greet her, his features impassive, her heart gave a ridiculous and thoroughly inexplicable little leap.

'I decided to join you for breakfast,' he said without preamble.

Irritation at her own pleasure in seeing him made her voice sharp. 'How terribly gallant of you. Or is this simply another part of the take-over bid you appear to be making on my life?'

His dark eyebrows raised. 'Are you normally this sweet to your breakfast partners?' He asked coldly. 'Perhaps that would explain the lack of a permanent one in your life.'

She flinched, stung by his verbal whiplash. But even as she opened her mouth to retort, she spotted the receptionist watching the exchange with unconcealed interest. 'I'm just about to go in to the dining-room,' she said firmly. 'You're welcome to join me if you wish.'

'I find that debatable,' he returned acidly. 'However, since this hotel serves a particularly fine breakfast, I'll put up with your childish petulance.'

She stalked ahead of him into the dining-room, silently fuming. Sweet heaven, the day had barely begun and they were at loggerheads already. How was she supposed to survive days, let alone weeks in his company without being driven to physical violence? Not that it would make much impression on him, she reflected with a touch of wry humour as she looked at his magnificent frame across the table. If she were to attack him it would be tantamount to a kitten attempting to savage a powerful lion.

'Something amusing you?'

She shook her head, swiftly suppressing the faint smile curving her lips. 'Nothing at all. It simply occurred to me that people condemned to the gallows normally enjoy a magnificent last meal. Is that why you've come here this morning—to watch me have mine?'

If he was surprised by the question he didn't show it. 'What makes you think you're condemned?' he countered.

This time her smile was sardonic. 'How could I think anything else? You've clearly got something to prove, and I don't believe you'll rest until you have proved it—using me to do so. And you don't strike me as the kind of man who would give any quarter.'

His features darkened perceptibly. 'Just what is it you believe I intend to prove?' His voice was strangely quiet, but she wasn't fooled. She was playing with fire, yet even being aware of that wasn't enough to make her draw back from the consuming flames.

She managed with an effort to shrug her shoulders nonchalantly. 'How should I know? Perhaps you see our documentary as a perfect vehicle for your own ends. But I should tell you, Mr MacLennan——' She was interrupted by the arrival of Margery Wilson, bearing a silver coffee-pot.

'Now, then,' the older woman said briskly, 'I thought I'd bring you this to keep you going till your meal arrives. I assume it'll be the full breakfast for you, Luke?'

He nodded, sending her a teasing smile that somehow twisted Clancy's insides. It was a million miles removed from any of the mocking smiles he'd given her. What must it be like to look into those eyes with their changing shades of grey and see such warmth, such affection? She looked away, unable to cope with this unexpected side of the man.

'All the trimmings, Margery,' he said. 'And tell Chef not to stint on the bacon.'

She chuckled. 'He won't. Not when I tell him it's for you.' She turned her eyes on Clancy. 'And what about you, Miss Hall? What can I bring you this morning?'

Clancy closed her eyes for a brief second, all too aware of the dilemma facing her. Any faint appetite she might originally have had this morning had vanished as soon as the receptionist had told her Luke was in the hotel. She couldn't even hope to face up to one of the gargantuan platefuls Margery had attempted to place before her the previous day—yet if she asked for her usual toast and coffee Luke and the waitress would probably join forces to come down on her like a ton of bricks.

She opened her eyes to see Luke watching her curiously.

'Well, Clancy?' he demanded. 'What's it to be? The chef here is a wonder—he can whip up just about anything you care to ask for—from waffles with maple syrup to kippers. Just name it.'

She'd been about to compromise and request a simple poached egg on toast, but the very suggestion of waffles and kippers brought back all the old waves of guilt, making her feel faintly sick.

'Just the same as yesterday, please,' she said firmly.

The waitress was clearly about to remonstrate, but Luke laid his hand on her arm, forestalling her protest.

'And just what exactly was that, Clancy?'

'Toast and coffee!' Margery cut in disgustedly before Clancy had a chance to open her mouth. 'Not enough to keep body and soul together.'

Luke's grey eyes bored into her. 'Why, Clancy?'

She felt the full force of their dual challenge bearing down on her and did her best to meet it, tossing her head defiantly.

'Haven't you ever heard of cholesterol? The kind of breakfast you're about to have is loaded down with the stuff.' She deliberately made her voice scathing. 'Fried eggs, fried bacon, fried sausage, fried bread—this may come as news to you, Mr MacLennan, but such fare isn't good for you.'

'I suppose you'd prefer a delicate little dish of beansprouts and lettuce,' he shot back. 'Nouvelle cuisine, isn't that what they call it?'

'At least meals like that won't lead to a heart attack,' she retorted.

'No, they'll simply let you fade away to a shadow.' He paused, his eyes narrowing thoughtfully. 'Is that what this is all about, Clancy? Are you so hung up on your figure that you're prepared to starve yourself to stay fashionably thin?'

He was so far from the mark it was almost laughable, yet even as she was about to scornfully deny the allegation she stopped herself. To tell him the truth would be to open the floodgates on all the pain she'd been suppressing so vigorously. She couldn't cope with that—not yet, and certainly not with him.

She shrugged, not quite managing to meet his eyes. 'As I believe someone once said, there's no such thing as being too rich or too thin.'

His lips thinned to an angry white line. 'Try telling that to those who have neither riches nor food,' he gritted out. 'And stop being a spoilt little brat.' As Clancy recoiled from the venom in his tone he turned back to the waitress, who'd been listening intently. 'Bring her scrambled eggs on toast,' he ordered. 'And tell Chef to make sure he uses only polyunsaturated fat.'

As Margery scuttled away he shot Clancy a fierce glance from beneath gathered eyebrows. 'There, will that satisfy the calorie-counter that passes for a brain with you?'

'How dare you?' Pushed nearly to the limit of her temper, she glared furiously back across the table. 'You have no right to...'

'No right to ensure you're well enough fed to stand up to what I have planned for you?' He shook his dark head impatiently. 'I have every right, since you don't appear to have enough sense to do it for yourself. Look, Clancy, I have little patience with this female obsession about weight. As far as I'm concerned, if people were to simply get out and use their bodies as they were intended to be used instead of lazing about in front of television sets, they'd have nothing to worry about.

'In any case——' he grinned lazily, throwing her completely off-balance with the abrupt change of mood '—I like to see a curvaceous woman—one who's not afraid to be softly feminine.'

'One with ample breasts and good child-bearing hips, you mean,' she hissed back, unhappily aware of her own boyish slenderness. 'One built to satisfy the typical male fantasy. The type you'd see in tabloid newspapers.'

A faint derisory smile touched his lips. 'Why not? Haven't you ever heard the old saying that man is made for war and woman for the recreation of the warrior? Most warriors would prefer something warm, soft and welcoming after a hard day in battle.'

A spurt of anger fierce and intense as a flame flared within her, sending a rush of colour to her pale skin. Only a lifelong abhorrence of making scenes in public places prevented her from picking up the nearest heavy object to hand and flinging it at him.

'What's wrong, Clancy?' he said, his voice soft and taunting. 'Does such a sentiment go against the grain of your feminist beliefs?'

'You know perfectly well it does,' she shot back. 'It's nothing less than despicable to suggest that women were put on this earth purely for the amusement of men.'

'Then prove I'm wrong,' he said calmly. 'Accept gracefully that you have limitations at present and work to overcome them. But give yourself a fighting chance to do so—if you refuse to eat properly, you won't stand a cat's chance on those mountains. Furthermore, I won't even let you try.' He looked up with a grin as the waitress returned with their meal. 'Thanks, Margery. This looks wonderful as always.'

Clancy looked at the plate set before her, waiting with resignation for the usual rush of nausea. To her amazement she felt hungry instead—the first pangs of hunger she could remember in weeks. She picked up a fork and tentatively began to eat, the scrambled eggs tasting light and fluffy in her mouth.

'You should get angry more often,' Luke commented quietly as she cleared the plate. 'It's brought a glow to your skin and your eyes are sparkling—and it's even given you an appetite. Anger's obviously good for you.'

Since her mouth was too full to retaliate, she contented herself with scowling across the table at him. But even as she did so, a wayward little bit of her soul couldn't help but wonder if it was really anger that had put the glow in her cheeks and the sparkle in her eyes—or Luke.

'So—what form of medieval torture do you have in store for me today, Mr MacLennan?' She gave him her most ingenuous smile as they left the dining-room. 'The rack, perhaps? Or are you going to start me off gently with thumbscrews?'

If she'd hoped to rile him, she was doomed to disappointment as his features remained impassive.

'We're going for a walk,' he said calmly.

'A walk?' She turned wide, incredulous eyes to him. 'A walk? After all that nonsense about making sure I ate enough to face the rigours you had in store for me—we're going for a walk?'

'After which we're going to the local leisure centre,' he continued as if she hadn't spoken. 'But I don't think it would be a good idea to launch straight into a work-out after a meal, do you?' Without waiting for a response, he strode off towards the front door and she was forced to follow, muttering savagely beneath her breath. She soon stopped muttering, however, forced to save her breath for the exertion of simply keeping pace with his long legs. If she'd been under any illusion that they were heading off for a gentle stroll, they were soon dispelled.

'You didn't actually mention we'd be race-walking,' she said caustically, practically forced to break into a jog to stay abreast of him.

He glanced down, amusement glinting in his grey eyes. 'Breaking into a sweat already? That proves you're not fit—we can't have gone more than half a mile.'

'Maybe so, but I'd hazard a guess we've broken the world speed record.'

He grinned heartlessly. 'No point in ambling along. You need to get your lungs and legs working.'

'Oh, they're working all right,' she muttered ungraciously. It didn't help to know he was being proved right—she was unfit. Not drastically so, and with luck it wouldn't take long to recover what she'd apparently lost in the weeks since returning to Britain, but certainly not fit enough to cope with clambering around chilly mountainsides.

As they continued walking she realised he'd eased his pace fractionally and was grateful for it, though wild horses wouldn't have dragged the admission from her. She wasn't about to give him the opportunity to lecture her all over again. Still, as she found a second wind from some untapped reserve, she found she was enjoying the walk—or would have in more congenial company. The scenery now they'd left the town behind was spectacular, filling her eyes with its magnificence and bringing a strange sense of peace to her soul.

'All right?' He slanted a questioning look in her direction. 'We can stop for a rest if you're labouring. I don't want to burn you out on the first day.'

She glowered darkly back at him, instantly losing the serenity she'd been savouring just a few moments before.

'There's no need to patronise me,' she returned acidly. 'I'm not about to keel over in a dead faint at your feet, though I'm quite sure you'd love it if I did just that.'

Irritation tautened his finely carved features as he stopped in his tracks and turned to face her.

'Meaning what exactly?'

She bit her lip, belatedly wishing the words back. Now she was in for yet another confrontation, and she had only herself to blame.

'Meaning just what I've been saying all along—that you're out to prove some kind of a point, and you're using me to do it.' As if squaring up for battle she planted her hands on her hips, her expression mutinous. 'I think you'd love me to beg for mercy—but you'll wait a long time, Mr MacLennan.'

He eyed her assessingly, his gaze roaming lazily over her slight figure, and heat flooded her cheeks beneath his scrutiny.

'Such a small frame to house such antagonism,' he said musingly. 'And such a shame to sully those perfect lips with such bitterness. Yet those self-same lips can also taste sweeter than mead. Which should I believe, Clancy?' He took a step towards her and instinctively she backed away, her eyes widening in alarm.

'Don't you dare touch me!' she spat. 'I've had quite enough of your Neanderthal tactics, thank you.' Even as she spoke a ripple of excitement coursed through her veins, stunning and infuriating her with its intensity. 'You mauled me quite enough in that lay-by. But you won't do it again.'

'I mauled you? Is that really how you'd describe it?'

He was toying with her and she knew it, but there was no way she could back down now without losing face completely. Again.

'Is there any other way to describe it?' In total contradiction to the anger burning deep within her, her voice sounded positively glacial. 'You quite blatantly took advantage of your superior strength to simply do what you wanted, ignoring any wishes I might have.'

He shook his head slowly, a faintly scornful smile creasing the corners of his mouth. 'How well you lie,' he said softly. 'But are you lying to yourself as well as to me?' He lifted one hand and, as if the world had gone into slow-motion, she watched it come closer and closer to her face. She could have evaded him, could have knocked his hand away, but she was rooted to the spot, mesmerised by his fingers as they breached the gap between them. When she finally felt their coolness on her heated cheek, she closed her eyes, knowing she was trembling beneath his touch, but unable to do a thing about it.

'Don't do this,' she groaned huskily.

'Do what, Clancy?' His fingers were barely touching her, their caress feather-light on her skin, yet rivers of flame were igniting in her blood. 'Maul you? Open your eyes, Clancy. Look at me.'

Devastated by her own weakness, she obeyed the softly spoken command, only to find herself gazing into the smoky depths of his eyes, depths that threatened to consume her. She wanted to move, wanted desperately to flee from a danger she couldn't even have put a name to, but she was immobilised, hypnotised by his very nearness. Only his hand was touching her, yet she was gripped by a longing to feel his entire body pressed along her own, hard and powerful. His fingers cupped her face and he grazed his thumb along the soft fullness of her lower lip. Unconsciously she touched her tongue to his thumb and he smiled knowingly.

'See how I use my superior strength to dominate you, Clancy?' he murmured softly. 'See how you struggle against me?'

She tried to shake her head, but co-ordination had fled and she could only gaze helplessly back at him through unfocused eyes.

'Tell me what you want, Clancy. Do you want me to accept the invitation I see in those pretty hazel eyes, to take you in my arms, to caress your soft white skin, to kiss those perfect lips?'

In that moment she came close to losing all notion of identity, all memory of the enmity she bore him, aware only that the central, innermost part of her soul was crying out in recognition of its mate. Ironically it was that cry of recognition, devastating as it was, that gave her a strength born of desperation, and she was able to pull away from his hand, even though the pain of it was almost physical in its intensity.

'Don't ever do that to me again,' she whispered savagely, through lips still trembling from his touch. 'For some warped reason of your own you're trying to humiliate me—but I won't let you! Do you hear me?'

He nodded, his eyes dark and unfathomable. 'I hear you,' he murmured. 'I hear the voice of a scared little girl who's afraid of the grown-up feelings in her body.'

Released from his touch and marginally more in control of herself, she was able to glare back at him.

'It hasn't even occurred to your arrogant soul that I might be revolted by your touch,' she hissed. 'Just because I haven't flung myself at your feet and begged you to take me, you assume I must be scared. Well, you're wrong. All the other women round here may idolise you, heaven help them. But you'll never count me among their number.'

'We'll see, my little spitfire.' His smile was totally unrepentant. 'We'll see. Now——' he glanced at his wristwatch '—I think you should have successfully walked off breakfast. We'll head for the leisure centre.'

Frustration bubbled within her like a volcano about to erupt. He was coolly and masterfully manipulating her—dangling her like a puppet by its strings. It was a sensation she'd never known before, and for the life of her she couldn't begin to work out how to deal with it. Anger, as she'd already discovered, was futile. In the face of her fury he simply smiled that lazy smile, clearly unaffected by her ire. She'd never met a man like Luke MacLennan before—had no weapon in her armoury capable of defeating him. But she'd find one, she swore silently as she fell rebelliously into step at his side. If it was the last thing she ever did, she'd find one.

The leisure centre was a fairly new building, another facility clearly built for the benefit of the tourists, and relatively quiet now that the peak holiday period was past. Clancy couldn't help but notice that everyone they encountered in the centre's foyer seemed delighted to see Luke, all of them greeting him jovially. As for the women—they positively purred like happy cats in his presence, she thought grouchily, as one middle-aged matron who should surely have known better batted her stubby eyelashes at him.

'The female changing-rooms are over there,' he pointed over to the left. 'I'll meet you in the gym.'

'If you can make it through the ranks of your adoring fans,' she muttered testily.

He raised one jet-black eyebrow in amusement. 'Do I detect a note of jealousy there, sweet Clancy?'

'Jealousy?' She shot him an incredulous look. 'What on earth could I possibly have to be jealous about?'

The lazy grin she was coming to recognise curved his lips and she clenched her hands into fists at her sides, irritated with herself. When would she ever learn to keep her big mouth shut?

'I haven't the faintest idea,' he returned mildly. 'Why don't you tell me?'

Completely at a loss for an answer, she summoned up her haughtiest look and whirled round on one heel, stalking off towards the changing-rooms with a ramrod-straight back. Hearing the sound of his knowing laughter behind her did nothing to sweeten her mood.

Still brooding darkly, she changed quickly into the black leotard and leggings she'd collected from the hotel en route to the leisure centre, pulling a pair of brightly coloured leg-warmers over her slender ankles.

Becoming aware that someone was watching her, she glanced up into warm and friendly brown eyes twinkling in a pretty though slightly plump face framed by a fluffy cloud of light brown curls.

'Hi,' the woman said cheerfully. 'I saw you come in with Luke. I'm Lacey Bennet.' She held out her right hand and Clancy shook it warily, wondering what was coming next. The woman seemed nice enough—but somehow everything to do with Luke MacLennan seemed to put her on her guard.

'Hello, Lacey. I'm Clancy Hall.'

The brown eyes held a hint of speculation. 'Are you a friend of his?'

'Not exactly,' Clancy hedged. 'That is, I haven't known him for very long.'

'What's to know?' Lacey smiled widely. 'To see that man is to love him—or at least to lust after him. Don't you think he's just the most perfect specimen ever created?'

Almost despite herself Clancy chuckled, enjoying the woman's blithe disregard for the proprieties. 'He is attractive,' she admitted, finding an unexpected pleasure in being able to say the words out loud.

'Attractive?' Lacey rolled her eyes heavenwards. 'Hell, Clancy, my pet rabbit's attractive—Luke MacLennan is a solid-gold hunk! It would be worth getting lost on the mountains just to be rescued by him. In fact——' she leaned forward conspiratorially, even though they were alone in the room '—I sometimes suspect some women do just that! Not that it makes the slightest difference.'

Clancy frowned, not understanding the cryptic remark. 'What do you mean?'

'Just that the man's a veritable Scarlet Pimpernel, my dear—totally elusive. Ask any woman under the age of forty in the county—they've probably all tried exercising their wiles, but he won't be caught.' She slid Clancy a slyly assessing look. 'Unless you know differently, of course.'

'Me?' Clancy's hazel eyes widened to their fullest extent as she shook her head vigorously. 'I'd rather catch a bad dose of flu than Mr MacLennan!'

Lacey laughed even though she clearly didn't believe a word of it. 'Frankly the symptoms would probably be very similar in both cases—though if the prescription for Luke called for a lot of bed-rest it would be worth suffering!'

Clancy was still laughing as they walked together into the gym, but the laughter froze in her throat when she caught sight of Luke talking to one of the attendants. In jeans and sweatshirt he cut an impressive figure, but nothing could have prepared her for the sight of him in cut-off denim shorts and T-shirt. Lacey Bennet had hit the nail right on the head, she thought dazedly—in purely physical terms, at least, the man was a solid-gold hunk.

Unable to deny herself the pleasure, she let her eyes roam over his magnificent frame from his broad shoulders to his powerful chest with its lavish pelt of silky black hair. She swallowed hard as she forced her gaze past the shorts riding low on his hips to his muscular thighs.

At her side Lacey gave a knowing little smile. 'What were you saying about flu?' she murmured. 'Looks to me as though you could be running a temperature right now!'

Before she could answer, Luke caught sight of them at the door, a smile creasing his features as he spotted Clancy's companion. He strode over to greet them, bending to kiss Lacey on the mouth. She quite blatantly made the most of it, reaching up to twine her arms around his neck and pressing her leotard-clad body against him.

'Steady, girl!' He was laughing as he released himself from her clinging embrace. 'I'm supposed to be warming-up, not overheating!'

Clancy felt an inexplicable little pang deep inside. It was obvious from the teasing exchange that the two were old friends, and even though Lacey had been provocative she was clearly just being playful. What must it be like to be so free and easy in his company? she wondered wistfully, then dismissed the thought abruptly. She wasn't even sure she liked Luke MacLennan, for goodness' sake. OK, she was attracted to him on a purely physical level, but she wasn't about to let that overrule her head.

'I really don't wish to interrupt,' she cut in stiltedly, 'but perhaps you could tell me where you want me to start on this fitness assessment.'

Luke's eyes narrowed irritably, but Lacey was apologetic.

'You're quite right to butt in, Clancy. I know I monopolise Luke quite shamelessly, but really, can you blame me?'

Clancy could do nothing but offer a faint smile, totally stumped for an answer to such a leading question. Even after knowing Lacey for just a few moments it was clear the woman held no malice in her soul—indeed, she was simply inviting Clancy to be as playful with Luke as she was being herself. But for the life of her she couldn't manage it. To her amazement it was Luke who came to the rescue.

'You'll have to excuse us, Lacey,' he said with a smile. 'Clancy's going to go through a fitness test, and I want to see how she gets on.'

'You mean you're going to watch?' Dismay at the very idea made her blanch. 'I thought you were intending to do a work-out of your own.'

'I can do both.' His eyes challenged her to argue further, but before she could even open her mouth Lacey cut in again.

'She looks pretty fit to me! Just look at that lovely lithe little body.' Clancy suffered agonies as two sets of eyes blatantly assessed her figure. 'Half the women who come in here would gladly sacrifice their husbands' bank balances to look like Clancy. Including me.' She looked disparagingly down at her own ample curves.

'There's a big difference between being skinny and being fit,' Luke pointed out.

'Now wait just a minute!' Cut to the very quick by his dismissive description of her slender frame, Clancy glowered up at him. 'I won't stand here and be talked about as though I were nothing more than a lump of meat.'

'Albeit a very lean lump of meat.' Lacey clapped one hand to her mouth, her brown eyes twinkling apologetically. 'I'm sorry, Clancy, you're quite right. It was extremely bad-mannered of us. Go on—do your test. I'm sure you'll pass with flying colours.'

Clancy gritted her teeth as Luke took her over to meet the attendant he'd been talking to earlier, wishing she could be one-tenth as confident as Lacey. No matter how much she kept telling herself it was ridiculous to fret, she couldn't help but view the approaching ordeal with trepidation. The young attendant was reassuringly sympathetic, however.

'This is nothing more than a simple programme to assess the state of fitness you're at currently,' he explained. 'From the results I'll be able to work out an exercise programme for you.'

She nodded. 'Fine. Where do we start?'

He gestured towards the various pieces of gym equipment. 'By going round those.' His boyish features relaxed into a grin. 'And don't look so worried—they don't bite.'

Painfully aware of smoky-grey eyes watching her every move, Clancy dutifully made the rounds of the various machines, lifting, stretching and twisting according to the instructions given. It wasn't long before a faint sheen of sweat was glistening on her forehead, but to her relief she found she was able to cope reasonably well with the demands of the equipment.

She was even beginning to feel quite pleased with her own achievements when she was thoroughly distracted by the sight of Luke going through his own work-out. His features set in concentration, he looked like a sleek and magnificent animal, muscles rippling beneath skin still bearing the last of a golden summer tan. Swallowing hard against a giddying rush of adrenalin, she looked hastily away, only to find herself gazing into Lacey's brown eyes across the room.

It was clear from the woman's knowing look that she'd been watching Clancy watch Luke, and when she gave a teasingly sympathetic wink Clancy felt her stomach muscles clench. Now, despite all the protestations she'd made, Lacey had doubtless marked her down as yet another member of the Luke MacLennan adoration band, and the knowledge rankled unbearably.

CHAPTER FIVE

'NOT bad, Miss Hall, not bad at all.' The attendant nodded slowly as he looked over the notes on his clipboard. 'I'd say with a regular exercise regime you could be up to peak fitness in a relatively short space of time. It helps of course that you're not carrying an ounce of excess weight.'

Try as she might, Clancy couldn't resist sending a tiny smile of smug triumph winging its way in Luke's direction.

'Having said that, however,' the young man went on, 'you really should think seriously about your diet. I'm just a little concerned about your stamina. You're certainly agile, but I feel you could tire easily. I'll give you one of our diet sheets—you don't need to stick to it rigidly, of course, but you might pick up a few tips from it.'

Her moment of pride vanishing as quickly as it had come, Clancy took the proffered piece of paper as graciously as she could.

'Thank you very much,' she said stiffly. 'I'll see what I can do.'

'You'll do a whole lot better than that,' Luke said firmly. His expression was determined as he nodded towards the attendant. 'I'll see to it personally.'

If she'd as much as glanced in his direction then, she'd have hit him. She'd never been driven to violence in her entire life, but now she was all but consumed by need to lash out against his easy assumption that he could tell her what to do. It was equally infuriating to discover that one tiny part of her actually wanted to obey. Well, she'd never allowed any man to dominate her, and she wasn't about to start now.

'I'm quite sure I'll be able to manage by myself,' she said with saccharine sweetness. 'A few notes on nutrition shouldn't be beyond even me.'

Aware that Lacey was quite openly watching them from across the room, she managed to dredge up a bright smile for the young man. Then, without as much as a glance at Luke, she headed for the dressing-room to shower and change. The warm water cascading over her skin helped to calm her down a little bit, but irritation returned in buckets as she spotted Luke at the main entrance to the leisure centre, talking animatedly to yet another beautiful woman.

As she approached, the woman gave a silvery, tinkling little laugh, clearly amused by something he'd said. The sound grated on Clancy's tightly strung nerves like nails drawn across slate, forcing her to grit her teeth. It was little wonder he was such a chauvinist, she reflected grouchily—he'd probably been charming the entire female sex ever since he'd lain in his cradle. And they, poor fools, had let him.

'I do hope I didn't interrupt a beautifully meaningful moment,' she said caustically as the woman walked away, having given Clancy no more than a cursory glance.

If he'd heard the comment he gave no sign of it, simply glancing at the watch on his wrist instead.

'Time for lunch,' he announced. 'And I know just the place.'

'I'd rather eat alone,' she returned, irritated that her barb had apparently bounced unheeded off his hide.

His features remained impassive, except for the barely perceptible twitch of a muscle in his cheek.

'What's wrong, Clancy? Are you scared I'll make you eat something? Afraid you might actually notch up double figure calories today?'

She tossed her head contemptuously. 'Quite the reverse. I'm looking forward to a pleasant meal, but frankly I'm afraid I'd suffer gross indigestion if I were forced to share it with you. In any case,' her voice dripped acid, 'I'm sure there must be any number of women who'd be delighted to gaze across a table at you. I'm just not one of them.'

'So that's it.' He nodded slowly, his eyes clearly amused. 'The little green-eyed monster is rearing his ugly head. Again.'

'Green-eyed monster?' Her scornful expression was tinged with wariness. 'I haven't the faintest notion what you're talking about. Again.'

'No?' One dark eyebrow quirked disbelievingly. 'Then let me give it a name, Clancy. Jealousy. You're jealous.'

'I'm what?' She all but shrieked the words back at him. 'Don't be ridiculous. I've never suffered from jealousy in my life.'

'Which is probably why it's hitting you with such intensity now,' he said sagely.

She took a deep breath, making a desperate but utterly vain attempt to quell the emotions churning inside her. 'There is nothing for me to be jealous of,' she said with exaggerated slowness, as if spelling the words out for a child. 'Nothing at all.'

'Who are you trying to convince, Clancy? Yourself, or me?'

She closed her eyes despairingly. She'd probably achieve more by hurling herself repeatedly against a brick wall than by trying to convince this man he could ever conceivably be wrong. But a deeply stubborn streak she hadn't even known she possessed refused to let her give in gracefully.

'Look,' she said firmly, 'for me to be jealous of anything concerning you would require first of all that I actually liked you. Since we both must realise that's not the case, it can't apply.'

His eyes darkened. 'You may not like me, sweet Clancy, but you want me.'

It took everything she possessed, but she managed to laugh. It wasn't quite the light, airily dismissive little laugh she'd hoped for, but, all things considered, it wasn't bad. She even managed to inject a note of amusement into her voice.

'It's obviously hard for you to accept that not every woman in the universe finds you devastatingly attractive,' she said. 'However, I can inform you here and now that such a being does actually exist, and she's standing right in front of you. You have absolutely no effect on me whatsoever.'

'None whatsoever?'

'None whatsoever.'

Unaccomplished as she was in the art of telling blatant lies, it was excruciatingly difficult to look straight into his grey eyes and say the words again, but for the sake of her own pride she had to make him believe it. Making herself believe it would be an entirely different matter.

He smiled. 'So it's not difficult for you to spend time with me?'

She shrugged. 'You're not someone I would willingly choose as a companion, but you have to become accustomed to dealing with all sorts.'

'So you could gaze across a table at me with total equanimity?'

'Absolutely.' Lulled by his seemingly artless line of questioning, she responded without thinking, only to see the trap as she fell straight into it.

'Good.' He had the air of one satisfactorily concluding a deal. 'Then let's go and have lunch.'

Clancy thumped down into the chair and reached for the menu. She hadn't spoken a word since she'd stalked out of the leisure centre with her nose pointing skywards, and as far as she was concerned it was a state of affairs that could continue indefinitely. If no words were exchanged, at least he couldn't rile her all over again.

That resolution dissolved as she ran her eye swiftly over the choice of food outlined on the menu. Then she glared at him accusingly.

'This is a health food restaurant.'

'And always has been.' He returned her gaze blandly. 'What did you expect?'

'Well, I expected . . . that is, I thought . . .' Thrown off-balance yet again, she was furious to find herself lost for words.

'You thought I'd take you to a steakhouse, or to a place where every dish comes loaded with stodge and calories,' he obligingly completed the sentence for her. 'Am I right?'

'Well, yes.' She frowned curiously. 'You're not a vegetarian, surely?' Then she shook her head. 'You can't be—not after the breakfast I watched you eat.'

'That doesn't mean I can't appreciate the value and nutritional goodness of vegetarian food.' He smiled faintly. 'Just because I'm a carnivore, it doesn't make me a savage. I thought you might find a vegetarian meal easier to handle than a plate of stodge.'

Her hazel eyes gazed at him; she was thoroughly nonplussed. After labelling him so firmly in her mind as an arrogant, self-satisfied chauvinist, it was disconcerting in the extreme to find he could be considerate. That he could actually take time out to think about her feelings and wishes. The discovery was warming and, because of that, strangely alarming too. It was bad enough that she was physically attracted to him. If she started finding there were things she could like about him too, it could be the thin end of a very hefty wedge—a wedge that could open up her tightly closed heart to something she wasn't at all sure she could cope with.

'You're looking at me as if you'd never seen me before,' he said lightly.

With an effort she pulled herself together. 'I'm just wondering what's behind this new ploy of yours,' she returned, deliberately making her voice sharp to conceal the way she was really feeling.

'No ploy,' he said easily. 'You seem to suspect I'm trying to fatten you up like a Christmas turkey, but that's never been the intention.'

'No?' Despite herself she couldn't help but smile at the mental picture his words created, a smile that turned of its own volition into laughter.

'Now I'm seeing something I've never seen before.'

Her eyes dancing, she sent him a quizzical look. 'What's that?'

'A genuine warm smile on your face. I was beginning to wonder whether you were physically capable of such an expression.'

Her smile vanished instantly. 'I'm perfectly capable of it,' she said stiffly. 'But I haven't found much to smile about where you're concerned.'

'Pity.' To her astonishment he reached across the table to trace the shape of her lips with one long finger. 'Your mouth was created for smiling. And for kissing—as I know.'

She flinched away from the disturbing warmth of his touch. 'I've never kissed you,' she bit out. 'I've simply suffered in silence as you kissed me. There's a big difference.'

Mockery glinted in his smoke-dark eyes. 'If what I tasted on those sweet lips wasn't the kiss of a woman returning in full measure what she was receiving, then I can't wait to experience the real thing.'

She fixed him with a baleful glare. 'Prepare yourself for a long wait.' To her relief a young waiter appeared at her side at exactly the right moment, almost as if she'd summoned him. For once it seemed she was to be allowed the last word on the matter. 'So what new rigours do you have in store for me this afternoon?' Waving away the basket of bread rolls he was offering, she picked up a fork. 'A ten-mile swim, perhaps? Or maybe just a gentle little marathon.' She waited for the all too familiar wave of revulsion to hit as she took her first mouthful of vegetable lasagne. It never came. Instead she was aware of a pleasantly hungry little gnaw deep in her stomach, a hunger she welcomed.

'You considered this morning to be rigorous?' He eyed her consideringly. 'That was a very mild workout.'

She bit her lip, knowing she'd been wrong-footed again. Knowing she'd done it to herself didn't help. 'I assumed you were easing me in gently,' she said stiffly. 'Lulling me into a false sense of security...'

'Before hitting you with the big one?' The faintest of smiles touched his mouth. 'But that would be irresponsible, Clancy.'

'And are you never irresponsible?' She gazed back at him, unaware that a faintly wistful look had crept on to her features. For some strange reason she had a sudden vision of Luke astride a powerful horse, hatless and with the wind blowing through his jet-black hair. It was a powerful image, one that sent a rush of something she couldn't even have given a name to eddying through her veins. Abruptly she shook her head, rattled by the image. 'Of course not. Stupid question. Forget I asked.'

'Why stupid?'

'Why?' She glared back at him, annoyed that he hadn't simply let the matter drop. 'Because you are the great Luke MacLennan—respected and admired, possibly even adored by all you meet. Well, almost all,' she amended swiftly, refusing to let herself be counted in with the rest. 'You couldn't possibly allow yourself to just let go, to throw caution to the wind. Whatever would people think?'

'They'd think what they already know,' he returned sharply, his features tautening. 'That Luke MacLennan is a human being. No more, no less. Furthermore, he's never believed himself to be anything else.' His eyes narrowed and she looked away from his penetrating gaze, the food turning to sawdust in her mouth as she automatically chewed and swallowed. 'Why do you insist on believing otherwise?'

'What makes you think I do?' she muttered uncomfortably.

'It's evident in every word you speak, every look you give me,' he returned, his even tones laced with a faint but undeniable anger. 'You've created a picture of me in your own mind—a picture which has no bearing on the truth, but which you're determined to hold on to.'

She blushed vividly, wondering what on earth he'd make of it if he knew just what sort of picture really had been in her mind just a few short moments ago.

'Why should I do that?' she countered, unknowingly toying with a linen napkin.

'You tell me,' he said shortly. 'On second thoughts, don't bother. You wouldn't tell me the truth anyway.'

She flinched, taken aback by the accusation. 'Are you suggesting I'm a liar?'

He shrugged. 'Not necessarily.' He pushed his empty plate away and leaned over the table, his eyes boring into her. 'I don't think you're aware that you're lying, because you're lying as much to yourself as to me—and perhaps to everyone else you meet.'

Incensed, she flung the napkin down on to the table and made to get to her feet, but before she could complete the move he grabbed her by the wrist. Only too aware of the interested eyes of the other diners, she subsided back into her seat. 'I haven't the faintest idea what you're talking about,' she hissed through clenched teeth. 'Furthermore, I think you've got the most incredible nerve—you don't know me at all, yet you presume to sit there and analyse me.'

'Have you ever had your palm read?'

She frowned, thoroughly bemused by his apparent *non sequitur*. 'What on earth does that have to do with anything?' She twisted her captive wrist in a bid to free it from his encircling fingers, but his grasp held firm.

'Have you?'

'Yes, I have, but I really don't see . . .'

'Were you impressed by what you heard?' He turned her hand over and spread her fingers open as his gaze dropped to her palm. 'Were you surprised that he should be able to look at your hand and know things about you that he couldn't possibly have known?'

'It was a woman,' Clancy returned stiffly, unsettled by the warmth spreading through her skin from the touch of his hand on her own. 'And yes, I suppose I was quite impressed.'

'Even though she was presumably a stranger, and yet she seemed able to look into your very soul.'

'Look, what is all this about?' Thoroughly rattled now, she glowered back at him, her eyes shooting sparks of defiance. 'Would you please just get to the point?'

Unmoved, he smiled—a strangely knowing smile that seemed to reach deep within her, threatening to dissolve away the barriers she'd built up against him. She shivered, a sudden and inexplicable fear of those all-seeing eyes finally giving her the strength to pull away from his grasp.

'You have a very expressive face, Clancy,' he said softly. 'I imagine your palmist probably ignored your hand and simply looked deep into your eyes. They say more than heart-lines or Mounts of Venus ever could.'

She massaged her wrist, still feeling the touch of his fingers branded on her skin. 'I suppose you're attempting to say you know all about me,' she said shakily, attempting to inject scorn into her words, but badly let down by a betraying tremor in her voice. 'Well, let me tell you, Mr MacLennan, you know nothing. I, on the other hand, can read you like a book—and it's not even a very interesting read.'

'You think not?' One dark eyebrow quirked upwards in lazy amusement. 'Then perhaps you should turn the page.' She jerked in surprise as he reached again for her hand and raised it to his lips. The touch of his mouth grazing her fingers sent a jolt through her body, making her gasp. He smiled knowingly as he released her nerveless fingers. 'You haven't even opened the book yet,' he said softly and the words seemed to ripple over her skin like a warm summer breeze. 'You're the researcher. You of all people should know that the truth often lies fathoms deep. It's up to you to find it—if you can.'

For long, endless moments she was held by the mesmerising spell of his eyes, lost in swirling mists of smoky grey. It took everything she possessed to finally break the spell and look away.

'Speaking of being a researcher, I think I'd better spend this afternoon doing some work,' she said crisply, her even tones a complete contrast to the turmoil she was suffering deep inside. 'I've promised to compile a dossier of facts and figures about the mountain rescue team.' She risked a glance in his direction. 'Perhaps you'd be good enough to tell me where I can find them?'

'You'll find everything you need in my office,' he said, his knowing look leaving her in no doubt that he'd seen straight through her ploy. 'But not today.'

She frowned, bridling inwardly at the calm authority in his voice. 'Why not?'

'Because I have other plans. This afternoon you're coming out on the fells with me.'

CHAPTER SIX

CLANCY slid gratefully between the cool sheets, wondering if she'd ever felt more tired in her entire life. Every bone, every sinew in her body seemed to sigh in relief as she lay unmoving, her eyes closing almost before her head had touched the pillow.

It had been an incredible afternoon. She'd been angered at first by Luke's cool assumption that he could change her plans apparently at a whim—angered still more by the fact that she could hardly protest, since he was only agreeing to do what she'd been asking for all along.

The anger had swiftly disappeared when he'd taken her to the big old country house he used as a base for the adventure courses he ran, and introduced her to the group of youngsters staying there for the week.

'Clancy,' he'd said gravely, 'I want you to meet Angus and the lads. Possibly the biggest bunch of tearaways it's ever been my misfortune to encounter.'

She'd been forced to swallow hard even as she was summoning up her brightest smile. Luke's 'tearaways' were all teenagers, all wearing typically boyish grins of sheer mischief as they looked back at her. And every one was handicapped. The youngest, a freckle-faced lad of about thirteen in a wheelchair, had sent Luke a speculative glance.

'Is Clancy your girlfriend, Luke?'

Luke aimed a mock-punch at the boy's shoulder. 'Why? Are you thinking of muscling in?'

Clancy chuckled along with the rest, even as she felt a scarlet flush stain her pale cheeks.

The youngster shrugged his narrow shoulders. 'I just might at that. She doesn't want to get landed with a wrinkly like you, does she?'

'I'll give you wrinkly, you young whippersnapper,' Luke growled. 'Just see which one of us is first up the mountain, Billy.'

Clancy blinked in surprise—surely he couldn't be serious? But Billy simply nodded, accepting the challenge.

'Fair enough. But it's not really a fair contest. I reckon you'll need a head start—on account of your great age.'

'Huh! We more mature citizens can still get the better of you infants.' Luke laid a friendly hand on the boy's shoulder. 'Now enough of all this talk. Are you ready, gang?'

The question was greeted by a chorus of approval and Luke nodded. 'Good. Then let's get going. But keep an eye on Clancy for me, lads—she doesn't know the ropes yet.'

A group of able-bodied helpers joined them as they made their slow and sometimes laborious way on to the fells, but, as Clancy quickly saw for herself, they only gave assistance when it was really needed. Most of the time the boys insisted on getting along for themselves if at all physically possible. The wave of pity she'd experienced on first seeing them soon changed to sheer unstinting admiration for their guts and determination, particularly since she was breathless and panting long before they showed any signs of exertion.

'Come on, Clancy,' Billy called to her as she struggled over one rocky patch. 'You can hitch a lift with me if the going's too tough for you.'

She angled him back a grin. 'No way, buster,' she retorted. 'If you can do it, so can I.'

Eventually they reached the top of a hillside and Luke held up one hand.

'OK, gang,' he announced. 'We're here.'

'Is this where we rest?' Clancy asked hopefully.

Luke sent a scandalised look towards the youngsters and rolled his eyes heavenwards, obviously inviting them to join in the teasing. 'Rest?' he echoed disbelievingly. 'Don't be ridiculous, woman. This is where the real fun starts.' He nodded towards the edge of the hill where the ground fell away sharply. 'We're going to abseil down there.'

'Abseil?' She took a few steps towards the edge and glanced back over her shoulder, her eyes wide and incredulous. 'Down there? Us?'

'All of us,' he returned firmly. 'Billy, you can go first. Show the lady how it's done.'

Lying warm and comfortable in the big double bed, Clancy gave a shudder as she remembered the moment of very real fear she'd gone through watching Billy, safely strapped into his chair, being lowered backwards over the edge of the hill. The fear hadn't been for herself, but for him, yet he'd gone into the unknown with a huge grin.

Feeling suddenly restless despite her exhaustion, Clancy turned over in bed, hugging her knees up to her stomach. She'd seen yet another side to Luke today as he'd moved easily and capably among those handicapped kids—never by so much as a single look betraying the concern he must surely have been feeling for them. He'd teased and laughed with them, but he'd treated them with just the same respect he'd have afforded able-bodied adults. Which come to think of it, she realised with a scowl, was more than he'd done for her.

He treated her as though she were a child most of the time, reprimanding her for not eating enough, taking charge of her exercise programme, sending her off to the sports shop with a list he'd written out himself. He probably didn't think she'd graduated to joined-up writing yet, she thought grouchily. Next thing he'd be checking she'd tied her shoelaces properly.

There again—he didn't always treat her like a child. Her cheeks grew warm with the memory of the times he'd kissed her. When he'd held her against his powerful body, he'd been holding a woman in his arms, had expected a woman's responses. And how had she responded? Like a gauche teenager, that was how!

With a disgusted snort she burrowed deeper beneath the bedclothes, desperately trying to blot out the mental images crowding her restless mind. It was impossible. Had it only been her mind she was trying to do battle with, she might just have succeeded—but her traitorous body was gladly answering to the clarion call of her imagination, her skin tingling at the very thought of being pressed against his. It came as no surprise when the telephone suddenly began to ring.

'Go away.'

'No way, kid!' Dan's cheerful tones echoed along the wires. 'Unless of course the very interesting vibes I'm picking up mean you're not alone, in which case I'll gladly——'

'Don't be ridiculous,' she cut in testily. 'Of course I'm alone. What do you take me for?'

'Wow!' The single word conveyed a wealth of meaning. 'You mean I'm picking up on thoughts alone? You've got a more vivid imagination than I've given you credit for.' He paused, his voice growing more serious. 'As to what I take you for—I take you for what you are: a beautiful young woman with a whole lot to offer, even though you seem determined not to realise it.'

'What do you want, Dan?' she asked wearily.

'Just touching base, sweetheart. Wondering what you've been getting up to...' he chuckled slyly '... though judging by your present state of mind I reckon you'd better give me the censored version.'

She pushed herself back up against the pillows and reached for the notebook on the bedside table. 'I've spent part of the afternoon working,' she said firmly, looking at the notes she'd made in Luke's office after they'd returned from the abseiling trip. 'And I've come up with some great material.' For reasons she couldn't explain even to herself, she was unwilling to tell Dan about the rest of the afternoon—didn't feel ready to share the experience, even with him.

'Good.' She heard the trace of disappointment in his voice as he reluctantly allowed her to change the subject. 'Spell it out.'

'For a start this mountain rescue team must be one of the busiest in the entire country, never mind this area.' She reeled off a list of statistics detailing the number of times the team had been called out in recent years.

'They've got an amazing success rate too,' she went on. 'They pride themselves in always being able to find their man—or woman, of course.'

'That's great. But we need more than figures, Clance. I want this documentary to probe the characters and personalities of the people in the team. I want to be able to show what makes them tick—what makes them go out in the worst possible conditions to save lives. Does any one team member stand out above the rest?'

She sighed. She'd been expecting the question, and, much as she'd have loved to deny it, there could be no gainsaying the part Luke had consistently played.

'I haven't met all the team yet,' she hedged.

'But?'

She pursed her lips ruefully—why did she even bother trying to conceal anything from her twin brother? 'But... from what I've read and heard so far, Luke MacLennan comes through loud and clear as the main man every time. He's a real driving force—an inspiration even.'

'MacLennan, huh? How was it you described him to me...? "Steely, determined, enigmatic, dynamic"—oh, yes, and "absolutely gorgeous", wasn't it? Add to that a dedicated and clearly charismatic leader—good grief, Clancy, no wonder your mind's threatening to go into overload.'

'Dan, your infantile brain is developing a most irritating habit of adding two and two together and coming up with a hundred and six. What makes you so convinced he's the one I've been thinking about?'

'I haven't heard you mention anyone else's name,' he retorted swiftly, then sighed, his voice heavily laden with reproof. 'Clancy, girl, when did you become so secretive? This is me you're talking to. We've always shared everything—the bad as well as the good. Why can't you open up to me about this guy? I know I've been teasing you, but that's just my clumsy way of trying to make you confide in me.'

Clancy pleated the candlewick bedcover between her fingers, uncomfortable at being put on the spot, and by Dan of all people. He was right, of course, they had always shared everything—until the Sudan trip. The burden she'd been carrying since then had been too heavy to share even with him. Now, for reasons she couldn't fully comprehend, she was trying to lie to him about Luke. She smiled ironically. Perhaps the real reason was that she'd been doing a pretty good job of lying to herself where Luke was concerned.

'OK, Dan,' she said resignedly. 'What do you want to know?'

'Everything,' he returned instantly. 'What sort of a man he is—and this time leave out the superlatives. Just give me the nitty-gritty. And . . .' he paused significantly '. . . I want to know how you feel about him.'

She took a shaky breath. 'Don't want much, do you? I don't know how I feel about him, and that is the truth. He infuriates me beyond belief, he tries to boss me around, he seems to think he knows me better than I know myself. He drives me crazy!'

'Sounds to me as if you're falling in love with him.'

'No way!' She all but shrieked the words.

'I thought you were going to be honest?'

'I am being honest,' she returned adamantly. 'I am positively, definitely and categorically not in love with him.'

'Why so vehement? You are allowed to fall in love, you know; it's not a federal crime.'

'I'd never allow myself to fall for someone like him.'

Dan laughed softly. 'I don't think it works quite like that. In any case, he sounds like God's gift to women.' He paused for a long moment. 'OK, I'll let up on you. What does he do when he's not rescuing people from snowy wastes?'

'He runs an adventure centre. Takes people canoeing, walking, mountaineering—you name it.'

'What sort of people?'

'Just about anyone,' she returned, thinking about that afternoon.

'Is he good with people?'

'Yes.' Whatever else she might say about Luke, she couldn't deny him that. The look on Billy's face as Luke prepared to lower him over the edge would stay with her forever—his eyes had been locked with Luke's as a silent but almost tangible flow of understanding passed between them. It had been a powerful, compelling moment, one she wished she could have captured on film. No one witnessing it could have been left in any doubt that in Luke MacLennan an incredible strength was combined in equal measure with compassion and understanding.

She found herself telling Dan about the afternoon then, her voice softly excited. 'Billy's just a kid, and he's been in that wheelchair all his life—he must have been terrified deep down. But you could see in his eyes that it was OK for him to go into the great unknown if Luke said so.'

Dan was silent for a long, telling moment. 'Reckon there could be a lesson for you there, sweetheart.'

She sighed. 'Don't go all philosophical on me. There's a big difference between abseiling down a hillside and falling in love.'

'Are you so sure? Seems to me they share a big something in common.'

'Which is?'

'Trust. I've never met your Luke yet, but if Billy was prepared to trust him with his very life, then he can't be such a bad bet to trust with your heart.'

Clancy managed with an effort to laugh. 'I prefer to keep my heart just where it is, thanks very much.'

'Could be your loss.'

More probably her salvation, Clancy thought grimly as she wished him goodnight a few moments later. It was all very well for Dan to be so wise—he'd never met Luke. He'd never seen the way every woman seemed to fall under his spell, their eyes almost glazing over with longing as they gazed at his magnificent frame.

How could you ever trust a man like that? The
temptations falling regularly into his path must be too
much for any red-blooded male to resist—and he certainly was a red-blooded male. No matter how hard
she might try to protest, Clancy knew she was far from
immune to him. He'd only had to touch her and she'd
all but fallen apart at the seams. But what could she
be to him other than yet another conquest?

If she were made of different stuff she might be
persuaded to simply grab whatever it was he had to
offer, for as long as he was prepared to offer it. But
at the end she'd be left with nothing more than the
bittersweet memories of a few wonderful nights in his
arms. No. He definitely wasn't a man to be trusted
with her heart.

It was hard work persuading her protesting body to
get out of bed the following morning, but Luke's
parting words from the day before finally provided
the impetus. 'I'll see you at the swimming-pool before
breakfast,' he'd said. 'Don't be late or I'll come up
to your room and drag you out of bed.' She didn't
doubt he meant every word.

He looked magnificent in swimming-trunks—a sight
to make any woman catch her breath in sheer delight.
His chest was broad and lavishly covered with a pelt
of jet-black hair, his legs long and muscular. Walking
round the perimeter of the hotel swimming-pool,
Clancy was resignedly aware of the way the other
women were looking at him. Even as she approached,
one bolder than the rest walked languidly to his side
and laid a hand on his arm and she was forced to

clench her teeth against a totally unexpected rush of jealousy.

For a lot less than two pins she'd happily have turned on her heel there and then and gone back the way she'd come, never stopping till she reached her room and maybe not even then. But it was too late. He'd already seen her, and a stiff-necked pride she hadn't even known she possessed reared up inside to prevent her from retreat. The woman beside him flicked a single dismissive glance in her direction as Clancy reached them, but his eyes ran lazily over her figure, a faint appreciative smile tugging at the corners of his mouth. She coloured vividly, more than a little self-conscious in the skimpy high-cut suit that was all the hotel shop had had left over from its summer stocks.

Resolutely refusing to let herself be cowed by the speculative watching eyes, Clancy took a deep breath and summoned up her most businesslike smile for the woman before turning to Luke.

'Good morning,' she said shortly. 'I trust I haven't kept you waiting?'

He glanced up at a clock on the wall. 'You're bang on time,' he returned blandly, though there was no mistaking the glint of amusement in his eyes. 'Apparently you didn't relish the thought of being dragged through the hotel.'

Clancy glowered back at him and the woman at his side gave a malicious little chuckle, clearly delighted by her discomfiture.

'I generally endeavour to be prompt,' Clancy said through tightened lips. 'I don't believe in wasting time if I can help it.'

'Well, don't let me interrupt,' the woman drawled, sending a sweetly sympathetic smile in Luke's direction. 'I can see you're on duty this morning, and I know you don't like to let pleasure get in the way of business.' She reached up to kiss his cheek, then strolled away, leaving Clancy floundering for a rejoinder.

'OK, let's get started.' If he'd even noticed any friction in the air he gave no sign of it, Clancy acknowledged with a trace of resentment. But then, he was probably all too accustomed to women making fools of themselves over him. Well, she wasn't about to join their ranks.

'Fine,' she returned curtly.

'How many lengths can you manage?'

She bit her lip. Even at her fittest, she'd never been a good swimmer. As a child she'd seen a man almost drown and it had left her with a fear of water she'd never managed to conquer. She was happy enough in the shallows, but the deep end of any swimming-pool was a nightmare. She glanced up at Luke and knew with a sinking feeling that she could never admit that to him. He already considered her a total weakling— she couldn't possibly hand him still more ammunition. Bolstering her courage, she looked him straight in the eye, her features set.

'As many as you want.'

'Start with three. See how you get on with that.'

She should have welcomed the reprieve—surely even she could manage just three lengths? Instead she was unreasonably irritated with his assumption that she couldn't cope with more. She tilted her chin defiantly. 'I'll do six.'

He gave her an assessing look, his eyes raking her face. Then he shrugged. 'Fine.'

Inwardly she was quaking as she followed him towards the water, unconsciously clenching and unclenching her fists as she silently berated herself for her ridiculous bravado. What on earth had made her say such a stupid thing? Even as she asked the question, she already knew the answer. It was because she wanted—no, more than that, she *needed* to prove herself to Luke. She needed to show him she was more than the weak female he seemed to believe her to be. And it wasn't even just because she wanted to show him she was fit enough to tackle the mountains, she realised with a wave of anguish. It went deeper than that, right to the very heart and soul of her.

She shivered slightly as she walked down the steps into the pool, feeling the tepid water lap round her body.

'Cold?'

She shook her head. The water wasn't particularly chilly, she was shivering through sheer nerves. 'Just getting used to it,' she returned as calmly as she was able.

He grinned heartlessly. 'The best way is to just jump straight in,' he advised. 'That way you get the shock over and done with quickly.'

As if to prove the point he disappeared beneath the surface, re-emerging a few seconds later, as slick and wet as a seal, drops of water glistening in his dark eyelashes.

'Come on,' he said. 'Let's get swimming.'

Her heart seemed to miss a beat as she watched him glide effortlessly away through the water, totally at home in an element that would forever be alien and inhospitable to her. He was a magnificent animal, she thought dully—no matter how much she might rail and fight against him, she could never hope to deny his strength and charisma.

With a heavy sigh, she launched herself into the water, gasping as its coolness hit her skin. With eyes closed and teeth clenched she concentrated all her efforts on simply propelling herself along the length of the pool, longing for the touch of the tiles that would tell her she'd made it safely to the far end. When her reaching fingers finally connected with the solid poolside, she swiftly swung her feet upwards and kicked off again, excruciatingly aware that she was in the deep end, with nothing but water and more water beneath her.

She might have made it—might have returned safely to the shallows but for a mischievous young boy who chose that exact moment to launch himself from a diving board, landing with an almighty belly-flop just inches away from her. Thrown completely out of the rhythm of her stroke, she strove to relax, knowing it was the only way to stay afloat. It was no use—even as she opened her mouth to scream, her body, tense and taut as a violin string, went under, the water closing over her head. Panic-stricken, she made a desperate bid to resurface, but managed to break through for only a second before going under again.

Terror was closing in, suffocating her, and she fought its fatal embrace, her legs and arms flailing wildly. It was only when her arms were pinioned firmly to her sides that she realised she was struggling with a would-be rescuer, and some remaining vestige of sense made her realise there was a very real danger that she could drown both of them. Even though it meant doing battle with all her own instincts, she managed to go limp and allow herself to be pulled back to the surface, taking great gasping breaths of air as she was lifted bodily from the water and laid on the cool tiles.

'Is she all right?' Anxious, querying voices echoed round her head.

'She will be.' The reply was clipped and grim. 'Move back, all of you—give her some air. Clancy, can you hear me? Have you swallowed much water?'

It was Luke—Luke whose strong arms had closed about her as she'd fought, Luke who'd dragged her to the surface and brought her to safety. Luke who'd saved her life. The realisation swamped her and she began to sob weakly, overwhelmed by it all.

'Open your eyes, woman. Look at me.'

She couldn't do it. Couldn't bear to look into those smoky grey depths and see the scorn they must surely hold.

'Leave me alone. I'm fine.' Her voice broke with the plea.

He swore briefly but with profound feeling, and hauled her none too gently into his arms, his body hard and powerful against her own. Shocked, her eyes flew open to see just a fleeting glimpse of his taut, forbidding features before she was lifted clean into the air.

'What are you doing?'

'I'm taking you to your room,' he returned curtly. 'Don't say another word, Clancy, or so help me I'll be tempted to fling you back into the water. Only this time I'll let you drown.'

Too stunned even to object, she subsided against him, burying her face in his neck as he strode long-legged from the pool area. In the hotel foyer, the young receptionist came scurrying up to Luke.

'I heard what happened! Shall I call for a doctor?'

He shook his head without breaking stride. 'She wasn't under the water long enough to do any real harm. Have some hot tea sent up to her room, would you? And a brandy.'

'I don't want any brandy,' Clancy muttered against his throat as he made his way upstairs, seemingly oblivious of her weight.

'The brandy's for me,' he returned tersely. 'Now be quiet.'

She wanted to rebel, wanted to cry out against his arrogant assumption that she would meekly obey his commands—but a single glimpse at his granite-like features effectively silenced her. She wasn't afraid of Luke—but in this mood she wasn't about to argue.

The chambermaid was cleaning Clancy's room when they arrived, but she didn't need to be told to leave, practically tripping over her own feet in her haste to obey Luke's unspoken command. He crossed the floor in a couple of strides and dropped Clancy unceremoniously on the bed.

'Right,' he barked. 'I want an explanation.'

'Explanation?' Marginally more in control of herself now that the terror had subsided, she looked up at him with a touch of the old defiance. 'What do you want me to explain?'

It was clear from the savage slash of his mouth that he was fighting hard to keep his temper on a tight rein. 'Why you omitted to tell me you can't swim.'

She hung her head. 'I can swim,' she returned, her voice so low he could barely hear it. 'But I'm afraid of the water.'

'Then why the hell didn't you tell me that?' His voice was like a whiplash, making her wince. 'In God's name, Clancy, you could have drowned.'

She was lost for words. How could she explain when she didn't really understand herself? Unconsciously she stroked her hand over the bedspread, unable to meet his eyes. Then she started violently as his hands grasped her by the shoulders, her eyes wide as she stared up at him.

'You could have drowned,' he said again, almost spelling the words out. 'It was obvious from the very second you started swimming that you weren't happy in the water. Why didn't you just say so, woman?'

The sudden shrill ringing of the telephone came as a blessed relief even though she knew the caller could only be Dan, and the prospect of explaining to him was less than pleasant. She reached for the phone but

Luke knocked her hand away and picked up the receiver himself.

'Yes?' His voice radiated grim hostility.

'Luke, give me that...' She reached again for the set, but he waved her away as though she were nothing more than an irritating fly.

'I'm afraid Clancy can't take your call. Who is this anyway?' He gave a single abrupt nod. 'I'll tell her you called.'

'How dare you?' Driven beyond the end of her tether, she made a wild lunge for him as he replaced the receiver. 'That call was for me! You had no right...'

'Since I saved your life no more than a few short minutes ago, I have all the right I need,' he returned, catching her flailing wrists easily. 'In fact, according to the tenets of some cultures, I now own you.' His eyes narrowed as she struggled wildly in his grasp. 'Though why anyone would ever want to own a spitfire like you is beyond me.'

Incensed, her eyes blazed sparks of fury as she scowled back at him. 'Dream on, Mr Wonderful Luke MacLennan,' she spat. 'You came to my rescue and I'm grateful for that, but don't start thinking it gives you any rights over me. I belong to no one but myself.'

'No?' His mood seemed to change, his eyes darkening to slate. 'Are you so sure of that?' His grip tightened momentarily on her wrists, then he gave one sharp tug and she fell against him, her defences shattered all over again by the feel of his naked chest beneath her cheek.

'Leave me alone.' Finding her hands freed, she reached up to grasp his shoulders, intending only to brace herself for flight. But his arms closed around her, enfolding her against him and she groaned, weakened immeasurably by the very touch of him.

'Let me go,' she moaned huskily. 'You have no right to do this.'

'No right?' He gave a short harsh laugh. 'You give me the right every time you look at me with those huge transparent eyes. You haven't even admitted it to yourself, Clancy J. Hall, but you want me.'

'No! You're wrong. I don't even like you.' But even as she struggled, the longing to give herself up to him, to surrender to the feelings pounding through her like waves on a shore, threatened to overwhelm her.

He thrust his fingers into her hair, cupping the back of her head as he bent towards her and her lips parted helplessly, their hunger for the taste of his mouth too great to be denied. His kiss made the last of her resistance disintegrate and she opened up to him like a flower freely offering its nectar to a plundering bee.

He pushed her back on to the bed, his body covering her own, and her bones seemed to melt within her as she felt the umistakable evidence of his desire pressing through the scant covering of her swimsuit.

All sense had fled, all realisation of time and place—even identity itself had become hazy as the elemental woman within her responded to the possession of her mate. Nothing else existed, nothing else was real but the touch of his fingers sliding the thin straps of her swimming-costume from her shoulders, and she arched up towards him, aching with the need to be touched. He dipped his dark head downwards and she groaned deep in her throat as he dropped a blazing trail of fiery kisses along her naked shoulders and finally down to her breasts, his lips closing over one hard nipple. She plunged her hands into his hair, holding him close, hungering for more of his touch.

Through a haze of longing she slowly became aware of a soft but insistent noise, and her entire body stiffened as she realised someone was tapping at the door. Luke gave a soft curse and pulled himself away from her. Her heart still racing within her, she watched as he answered the door, his face grimly set as he took possession of a tea-tray from the hapless porter, then closed the door firmly in his face.

'Saved by the bell, eh, Clancy?' He laid the tray on the bedside table.

'Thank God.' Horrified by the realisation of how close she'd come to losing control altogether in his arms, she glared up at him. 'Otherwise who knows what would have happened?'

He gazed at her for a long moment, his mouth twisting scornfully. 'Lying again, Clancy? Nothing would have happened that you weren't longing for—and you know it.'

Suddenly aware she was naked to the waist, she made a grab for a pillow, holding it like a shield against her. 'That's not true,' she hissed. 'You were using your usual caveman tactics, completely ignoring my wishes.'

He raised one ironic eyeborw. 'Ignoring your wishes?' He leaned closer and she shivered with the warmth of his breath on her skin. 'Your wishes were completely clear. You wanted me—wanted me to hear the pleas of your body. And, believe me, your body was pleading—loud and clear.'

He got to his feet and lifted the snifter of brandy to his lips, draining it in one swallow. 'One of these days you might find yourself having to grow up, Clancy. Maybe then you'll find the courage to face up to the truth about what it is you really do want in life. It'll be an interesting moment.' He turned his back on her then and strode towards the door, stopping at the last moment to turn back. 'I'll see you in the dining-room.'

Her hazel eyes widened incredulously. After all that had just happened, he expected her meekly to join him for breakfast? The man was truly beyond comprehension.

'Go to hell,' she returned, clearly enunciating each word.

He grinned heartlessly. 'I'll give you fifteen minutes,' he said. 'If you're not in the dining-room by then, I'll show you just how much of a caveman I can be. And something tells me your much vaunted equality would suffer somewhat if you were to be seen being dragged across the floor by the hair.' He cast a disparaging glance at her short crop. 'What there is of it.'

Unthinkingly she hurled the pillow she'd been holding at him, only remembering she'd been using it to cover her nakedness when his eyes dropped blatantly to her breasts.

'Thanks,' he murmured appreciatively. 'I've always enjoyed pretty scenery.'

It was only the sound of the telephone beginning to ring again that stopped her from launching herself at his throat.

CHAPTER SEVEN

CLANCY dropped her head into her hands with a deeply exasperated groan as she finally managed to get Dan off the phone. Why couldn't she just pack her bags and walk away from this place? she wondered despairingly. Or, to be more accurate and honest, away from Luke and the deeply unsettling effect he was having on her soul. Because she'd committed herself to a project, she reminded herself resolutely, and nothing would prevent her from seeing it through to the end, no matter how bitter the end might turn out to be.

Then she gave a hollow little laugh. Committed to a project, indeed—the awful but inescapable truth of the matter was that sheer stubborn pride wouldn't allow her to be driven away by a man, even one as devasting as Luke. Somehow she had to get through this thing, even though it was fast becoming the toughest challenge she'd ever faced.

He was already in the dining-room when she walked in, deliberately keeping her back ramrod-straight and her chin held defiantly high. He glanced at his watch as she wordlessly pulled out a chair.

'Made it with thirty seconds to spare,' he said. 'I'm glad to see you believe in being punctual. Or was the prospect of being dragged through the hotel by the hair simply too much for you to take?'

She sent him a withering glance. 'If you had as much as touched a single strand of hair on my head, I'd have taken extreme delight in asking the local policeman to make out a charge of assault against you,' she said coolly.

He raised one amused eyebrow. 'I'm sure Jim would have enjoyed that.'

'Jim?'

'The local policeman. My second-in-command on the rescue team.'

Bested yet again and unable to do a single thing about it, Clancy subsided with less than good grace into the chair, mentally counting to ten. No doubt news of her near-drowning would already have gone round the entire hotel, if not the entire village, and she wasn't about to give people any more to gossip about by throwing a tantrum at the breakfast table.

Concentrating on keeping her still uncertain temper on a tight rein, she barely noticed what she was eating until the waitress bustled up to clear the table.

'Well done, miss.' She nodded approvingly at Clancy's empty plate. 'That's the most I've seen you eat since you arrived. Luke is obviously having a good influence on you.'

If she'd been eating anything at that moment, she'd probably have choked on it. Instead she managed to muster up a weak smile. 'I think the Lake District air and lots of exercise probably has more to do with it——'

'Oh, come, come, Clancy,' Luke cut in reprovingly, the glint in his dark eyes clearly telling her he was enjoying her discomfiture. 'Surely you'll give me some credit for helping to reawaken your slumbering appetites.'

The innuendo in his words apparently passed clear over the waitress's head, judging by the innocently pleased smile creasing her plump cheeks. It didn't pass Clancy by, however. She glared back at him, her annoyance fuelled still further by the heat flooding her cheeks.

'You go too far,' she spat as the woman walked away. 'How dare you embarrass me like that?'

His broad shoulders lifted fractionally. 'Why be embarrassed by the truth? She was right—you have eaten more than you normally do.'

'It wasn't my appetite for food you were referring to, and you know it,' she shot back.

'No?' He propped both elbows on the table, steepling his fingers beneath his chin as he eyed her consideringly. 'Then you tell me, Clancy—what other appetite could I possibly reawaken within you?'

The faint blush staining her fair skin deepened to crimson as she floundered helplessly for a rejoinder.

'But perhaps that's not quite accurate,' he went on musingly. 'Perhaps I didn't reawaken anything— perhaps I brought it to life for the very first time. Is that the case, Clancy?'

She wanted to scream a denial back at him, couldn't bear to give him the satisfaction of believing he was the first man to stir fires in her blood. But she couldn't do it—couldn't tell such a barefaced lie. Instead she tossed her head contemptuously.

'What if you did? It's nothing to be particularly proud of. I've simply never had the time or the inclination to indulge in that sort of thing before. And frankly,' she forced herself to sound dismissive, 'I'm not in any hurry to try it again. It seems a vastly over-rated form of entertainment.'

'So you're a virgin.'

The bluntness of his statement took her breath away. For a long, speechless moment she could only stare at him, utterly taken aback.

'I really don't see that that's any of your business, Mr MacLennan,' she managed to sputter at last.

He gave a single nod as though in confirmation. 'You are a virgin.' His eyes were impossible to read as he studied her. 'Not very usual in these permissive times, but not unique. Any particular reason?'

He could have been discussing the weather, she thought dazedly, almost beginning to wonder if she was dreaming this whole ridiculous scene. Here they were, in the dining-room of a sedate Lake District hotel, still surrounded by other residents finishing breakfast, and he was proposing to indulge in a chat about her degree of sexual awareness. It couldn't be happening to her.

'Mr MacLennan——' she leaned forward, lowering her voice and making every word slow and deliberate '—as I believe I intimated just a moment ago, this is none of your business. It has absolutely nothing, zero, zilch to do with you. You have no right to ask. And I...' she sat back in her chair, folding her arms with an air of finality '...have no intention of telling you.'

He grinned lazily as he stood up from the table. 'Then I look forward to making the discovery for myself.'

'Not in a million years!' Outraged by his matter-of-fact reply, she leapt to her feet, almost overturning the chair in her anger. 'You may be able to get any woman you choose just by crooking your little finger, but I'm not one of your blasted harem—and I never will be.'

A mocking smile curved his mouth as he glanced round the room. 'You would appear to have thrown down a gauntlet, Clancy,' he drawled. 'And in public too.' His dark eyes glinted dangerously. 'So perhaps you should know—I never refuse a challenge.'

A faint *frisson* of fear tinged with an undeniable edge of excitement rippled over her skin. 'Even if it means taking me against my will?' she gritted out, no longer caring that people were watching and listening to their exchange. 'Because that's the only way you'll ever succeed.'

He shook his head. 'I don't believe that's true. Furthermore—neither do you.' He glanced at the watch on his wrist. 'Now, I suggest you take yourself off for a nice relaxing walk to work off that break-fast. I'll see you back at the pool in an hour.'

'The pool?' She'd been about to lose her temper completely, but his abrupt change of tack took the wind from her sails. 'The swimming-pool?'

'Correct.'

She shook her head. 'I'm never going near that pool again.'

'Yes, you are,' he returned firmly. 'In an hour's time.' Perhaps reading real fear in her eyes, he softened his expression fractionally. 'It's just like riding a horse, Clancy—when you've had a bad fall, it's best to get straight back into the saddle. You need to get straight back into the water otherwise the fear you already feel will escalate into a phobia. Only this time...' he fixed her with a piercing look that brooked no argument '...I'll be at your side the whole time. This time you're going to swim properly.'

When someone annoyed, infuriated and generally sent you round the bend as thoroughly and comprehensively as Luke MacLennan, it was hard to admit he might be right in anything, Clancy acknowledged grumpily as she made her way back to the dressing-room later that morning. But he had been right to make her get back in the swimming-pool—if she hadn't done it today, she'd probably never have been able to face up to anything deeper than a bath again.

'Clancy!'

Lost in her own thoughts, the unexpected sound of her own name made her jump, but she smiled as she turned to see a familiar plump figure bearing down on her. It was the friendly woman she'd met at the leisure centre.

'Hello, Lacey.' Genuinely pleased as she was to see her again, Clancy couldn't help but be slightly wary, wondering if the other woman really wanted to see her, or if she was simply cultivating a friendship in the mistaken belief that it would get her closer to Luke. Then she shook her head. She was becoming ridiculous—paranoid even. Lacey probably didn't have anything of the sort in mind.

'How's that gorgeous man?' Lacey's warm brown eyes twinkled mischievously as she reached Clancy's side. 'I saw him giving you a swimming lesson—you lucky thing!'

Clancy heaved a silent sigh. So much for the faint hope that one woman in the universe might possibly have something other than Luke on her mind.

'If you mean Luke, I'm sure he's perfectly well,' she returned a little coldly. 'Why don't you ask him yourself?'

Lacey pretended to flinch. 'Ouch! Touched a raw nerve, have I?' Unperturbed, she slipped her arm through Clancy's as they went into the dressing-room together. 'Anything you'd like to tell good old Aunty Lacey about?'

Looking into the irrepressible brown eyes, Clancy found it impossible to keep up her bad humour, and she smiled.

'That's better. Now come on—spill the beans.'

'There's nothing to spill.' She collected a towel from her locker, then frowned. 'Blast! I've forgotten to bring shampoo down with me. I'll have to go back to my room to shower.'

'Oh, no, you don't.' Lacey wagged a playfully admonishing finger. 'You can borrow mine. You don't get away that easily, my girl.'

Resigning herself to accept the inevitable, Clancy took the shower cubicle next to Lacey's.

'I heard about your little drama this morning. Is it true he really saved your life?'

'I got out of my depth. He hauled me out.'

Lacey gave a coquettish little chuckle. 'How wonderful! I'd love to find myself being rescued by those strong, muscular arms.'

'There was nothing very wonderful about it,' Clancy shot back. 'It wasn't deliberate, if that's what you're implying.'

There was silence for a moment and she bit her tongue, regretting her shrewishness. Lacey hadn't deserved to have her nose bitten off, but really the blanket adoration she kept finding for Luke was fast becoming too much for flesh and blood to bear.

She finished showering and walked back to the dressing area. Lacey was there already and she looked up with an apologetic smile as Clancy approached.

'I'm sorry,' she said simply. 'I realise I overstepped the mark.'

Clancy shook her head. 'I should be apologising, not you. I seem to be unduly touchy at the moment, but I shouldn't take it out on other people.'

The woman's smile returned in full force. 'Forget it. My skin's tough. However...' she tilted her head to one side as if studying Clancy '...yours is not. Call it an educated guess if you like, but I'd say you're in a bad way over Luke.'

She clapped one hand to her mouth, her eyes widening in self-rebuke. 'Lord, there I go again!' She held out one hand, like a child anticipating a caning from the teacher. 'Go on,' she said. 'Six of the best. I deserve it.'

Almost despite herself, Clancy began to laugh, feeling the strain of the morning easing in the other woman's company.

'That's better,' Lacey nodded approvingly. 'I get the impression you haven't been laughing very much recently. Is that because of Luke? You mustn't pay

too much heed to all the other women, you know,'
she went on, not waiting for a reply. 'I know it must
be hard for you feeling you're having to share him,
but he is the county's most eligible bachelor—you
can't really blame them for refusing to give him up
without a fight.'

'Give him up?' Clancy's hazel eyes showed her
confusion. 'What are you talking about?'

'Well, it's obvious, isn't it? The man clearly has
eyes only for you.'

Clancy shook her head decisively. 'You've got that
completely wrong. He's been spending a lot of time
with me, but only because he wants to ensure I'm fit
enough before he allows me to venture on to his
precious mountains.'

A mischievous smile played about Lacey's mouth.
'And you think he couldn't have got someone else to
do that? Luke runs his own adventure centre—he
could have put one of his staff in charge of looking
after you. You mark my words—he may not know it
himself yet, but he wants you.' She laid one hand on
her heart with a melodramatic sigh. 'And what that
man wants—he gets.'

Which was exactly what she was afraid of, Clancy
thought ruefully as they left the dressing-rooms
together. She couldn't even deny Lacey's claim—he'd
made it perfectly clear that he wanted her. Nor could
she lie to herself—part of her would give almost anything simply to give up the struggle and surrender to
what would surely be a glorious experience, one she
would never forget.

She couldn't do it—couldn't allow herself to give in to mere physical attraction. He wanted her, but only as another notch on his bedstead, and, no matter how strong the desire she felt for him, she wasn't about to become just another conquest.

'I haven't been able to get hold of you for days, woman! Where on earth have you been—and what have you been doing?'

Reaching down to lace up a pair of sturdy walking-boots, Clancy tucked the receiver between shoulder and ear. 'You may well ask, Danny boy. I've been doing just about everything you could possibly imagine—and all of it energetic.'

'Everything?' His laughter was slyly teasing. 'Don't forget, I can imagine quite a lot!'

'Drag your mind out of the gutter for once,' she returned amiably. 'I've been swimming, working out, walking . . .'

'Swimming?' Dan's astonishment came over loud and clear. 'But you've always been terrified of anything deeper than six inches.'

'Well, I'm not any more,' she returned, unable to keep a note of smugness from her voice. 'As of this morning I can now manage ten lengths of the pool.'

'Thanks to this Luke guy, I suppose.' There was no mistaking the faint note of irritation in his voice. 'How come he's managed to get you over your fear when I never could?'

She smiled, feeling a rush of affection as she realised her twin brother's nose had just been pushed slightly out of joint. She couldn't blame him for feeling a little peeved—he'd spent hours trying to coax her into the deep end of pools with no success. Somehow with Luke it had been different—he'd made her believe in herself, made her believe she was strong enough to face up to her fears.

'I'm just glad he has,' she returned lightly. 'The water's fun! Now I finally realise what I've been missing all these years.'

'Has the bold hero managed to initiate you into any other delights you've been missing all these years?'

'Dan!' The boots finally tied securely, she waggled her feet experimentally. 'I'm sure I haven't the faintest idea what you're talking about.'

'I'm sure you do. Come on, Clance, 'fess up. What's really going on between you and him?'

'You've always been able to read my mind,' she hedged. 'You tell me.'

'All I'm getting from your mind these days is a whole heap of confusion that tells me nothing.'

'Well, that's probably about as honest and accurate a response as you'll get.' It was true. Where Luke was concerned, her head really was, as Dan had so graphically put it, a whole heap of confusion. She hadn't dared investigate too closely into the state of her heart, preferring to keep it tightly under protective wraps.

The last few days, when it seemed as though he was never away from her side, had been exciting, challenging, demanding and utterly exhausting. He could switch from authoritative teacher to infuriating slave-driver to supportive ally seemingly in the blink of an eye. Just when she thought she was finally beginning to get a handle on him, he'd change again, leaving her as confused as ever.

One thing had remained infuriatingly constant, however, and that was his ability to make her go positively weak at the knees with just a glance. It was a response she fought hard to conceal, usually beneath a veneer of acid retorts. He must think her a real shrew sometimes, she thought regretfully, but sarcasm was one of the few weapons she could call on.

'Has he allowed you into the hills yet?'

'We're going for our first proper walk this afternoon and, to be perfectly honest with you, I can't wait.'

'Is that a fact? So where's the researcher I used to know and love with her famed capacity for total objectivity?'

Clancy bit her lip, knowing he'd be regretting the thoughtless remark. Her so-called objectivity had suffered a colossal blow in Sudan—a blow she wasn't at all sure it would ever recover from. But how could any feeling person remain objective in the face of such stark horror?

'I'm sorry, Clance.' Dan's voice came softly along the line. 'That was a stupid thing to say.'

'Hey, it's OK. Anyway, I know you're going to feel just the same way about this place as I do.' Her eyes grew strangely misty. 'Oh, Dan, it really is wonderful. I can understand why he loves the mountains so much—they're incredible. I can't wait for you to see them.'

'Well, you won't have to wait much longer. I'm planning on a trip up soon to do a spot of preliminary filming. See if you can sort out a couple of good photogenic areas for us.'

'That won't be difficult. Just about the whole Lake District is breathtaking.'

'Particularly if you're in breathtaking company, huh?' To her relief the teasing note was back in his voice. 'I'll look forward to seeing the place—and to meeting this amazing man.'

'Well, that's one way to describe him, I suppose,' Clancy muttered to herself as she laid the phone down a few moments later. But Luke MacLennan was so many things—amazing didn't tell the half of it.

'The other members of the team are getting together tonight in one of the local bars. It'll be a good opportunity for you to meet them.'

Clancy pursed her lips. If she'd had the strength she'd have caustically pointed out that she might just have had other plans, and frankly she didn't appreciate his taking it for granted that he could take over her evenings as well as her days. Since they were making their way up a particularly steep slope at the time, however, she needed every breath she could find, so she simply nodded.

'OK.'

Reaching a tricky spot, he stretched out one hand to help her. She eyed his fingers warily, knowing she could do with his assistance, yet all too aware that as soon as he touched her it would send the usual jolt of electricity surging through her. She should be getting accustomed to it by now, for heaven's sake, she told herself sternly—over the past few days he'd touched her a lot, though never in a way that could be construed as anything other than simply helpful. But her response was always the same—he only had to lay a casual hand on her shoulder and she was in danger of dissolving before his very eyes. She could only pray he hadn't noticed.

'Is there anything you want to know about them?' he asked, and she blinked confusedly, having temporarily lost the thread of the conversation as soon as he'd grasped her hand.

'Know?'

'About the team,' he said patiently. 'We were talking about them thirty seconds ago—remember?'

'Of course. I was distracted by the view for a moment,' she lied through her teeth, feeling relief and regret in equal measure as he released her hand. 'I want to know everything about them—what sort of people they are, what their jobs are, what makes them risk their lives on the mountains. Everything.'

He slid her a sideways look. 'Is that the researcher speaking—or you?'

She frowned uncomprehendingly. 'I don't understand what you mean.'

'Are you interested in them as people, or as characters for your film?'

She had to think about that one for a moment. 'Both, I suppose,' she said at last.

'That's honest, at least.' Reaching a more level piece of ground, he strode off and she was almost forced to break into a trot to keep up.

'You sound surprised,' she said a touch breathlessly when she finally drew level. 'Why wouldn't I be honest?'

He stopped and turned to look down at her. 'You tell me,' he returned cryptically. 'It seems to be something you find difficult.'

'I resent that! I am not a liar.'

He shrugged. 'You're certainly accomplished in the art of lying to yourself.'

Angered, she planted her hands on her hips and glowered up at him. 'Would you care to elaborate on that?' she said icily.

'Just look at yourself now.' He gestured with one hand at her stance. 'You're on the defensive, just as you habitually are with me—but it's a deliberately manufactured response.'

'"Deliberately manufactured"?' She made a show of seeming to examine the words, then shook her head. 'I haven't the faintest notion what you mean.'

'Haven't you?' He took a step closer and her eyes widened apprehensively, though she managed with an effort not to back away. 'Then let me explain. You deliberately go on the defensive to cover up the way you feel about me. It's a pretty good cover, too,' he went on, holding up one hand to stem the flow of her answering indignant retort. 'Except, that is, when I touch you, when the cover falls very sweetly to pieces.' The dark grey eyes regarded her steadily, yet with more than a hint of challenge. 'Can you deny that?'

'Of course I can deny it,' she shot back hotly. 'If I'm defensive it's because I don't want you to touch me. As for falling to pieces...' sparks of anger danced

in her eyes '...that, Mr MacLennan, signifies dis-
taste, not desire.'

'Prove it.'

'What?'

'You heard me, Clancy. Prove it.'

She was shocked into silence for a moment, left
floundering for a reply. He offered no help at all,
simply standing before her, an enigmatic smile playing
about his lips.

'This is ridiculous,' she said at last. 'You're playing
games. Well, you can play them alone. I won't have
any part of it.'

'Are you afraid?'

'What is this?' Backed into a corner, she gazed at
him incredulously. 'What are you trying to prove?'

'I'm not trying to prove anything,' he returned
calmly. 'I already know the truth. I'm trying to make
you face up to it as well.'

'And just what is the truth—or, rather, your version
of it?' She deliberately injected a sneering note into
her voice. 'No, let me guess. You think I'm just
another lovesick female aching to join your devoted
band. You think it's just some sort of silly female
pride that's keeping me aloof. Is that it?' Even as she
was hissing the words at him she was inwardly praying
he wouldn't realise how perilously close to the truth
they really were. 'All right, Mr MacLennan, I'll go
along with this idiotic charade if that's what it takes
to finally convince you you're wrong. What do you
want me to do?'

'Kiss me.'

If he'd suggested she strip to the skin and run backwards up Helvellyn she couldn't have been more astounded.

'I beg your pardon?'

The corners of his mouth twitched, though his expression remained solemn. 'You don't recognise the term? Perhaps you'd like me to give you a demonstration first.'

She shook her head vehemently. 'I think I can cope, thanks.'

'Very well,' he said gravely. 'How would you like me?'

Her eyes widened to their fullest extent. 'Like you?'

'Sitting? Standing? Lying on a nice soft bed of bracken?'

She knew what he was doing—knew he was blatantly manipulating her. She also knew she had only herself to blame—she could have turned down his ridiculous challenge. But deep down she was still gripped by a need, however foolish, to prove herself to him. Perhaps this would be the only opportunity she'd ever get to show she wasn't the weak and fragile female he believed her to be—the only chance she'd ever get to display her real inner strength.

Squaring up to him, she straightened her shoulders and took a deep breath. 'Standing will be fine.' Then as he stood waiting patiently she realised with a flare of irritation that she couldn't hope to reach up far enough to kiss him without standing on tiptoe, and that would be well-nigh impossible in heavy walking-boots. 'Perhaps you'd be good enough to bend your head a little?' she requested testily.

'I could lift you up,' he suggested helpfully.

She glowered darkly, ready to let fly at the slightest sign of mirth on his part, but he remained granite-faced. 'That won't be necessary. Just bend a bit.'

Obligingly he dipped his head towards her and she planted a fast, feather-light peck on his lips. 'There,' she said triumphantly. 'That should prove it.'

He shook his head. 'I don't think so.'

'But you told me to kiss you and I just did!'

'I don't believe that could by any stretch of the imagination be described as a kiss.'

'You didn't stipulate that it had to be a long kiss,' she remonstrated.

'I didn't say it hadn't to be. But if you're not confident enough of your ability to resist me...' He let the sentence trail away unfinished.

'Oh, for goodness' sake!' Exasperation finally drove sense and caution to the far winds and she flung her arms round his neck, pulling his head down towards her. For all of two seconds she thought she'd manage to see it through, with her eyes screwed shut and her lips clamped firmly together. Then his mouth moved beneath her own, warm and inviting, and she knew her mistake had been a fatal one. With everything she possessed she did battle internally with her own huge need for him. It wasn't enough. The longing to open up to him, to revel in the sheer joy of pressing against that hard, masculine body, was more than she could fight.

Barely even aware of what she was doing, she let her vice-like grip on his neck relax into an embrace, her fingers finding their own way into his thick black hair as she pulled him closer still. The tiny part of her brain that was still managing to function grew irritated with the number of clothes they were both wearing—the weather was cold enough to demand a lot of layers, but right now they were a wholly unwelcome barrier.

Any foolish, fleeting notion she might initially have entertained that she was actually in command of the situation had silently vanished as soon as his lips touched hers. She was boneless in his arms, her body's longing to submit far more powerful than her mind's wish to resist.

To her everlasting chagrin it was Luke who finally broke away, Luke who gently disentangled himself from her embrace to hold her at arm's length. Dazed by the onslaught of her own tumultuous feelings, she gazed up at him through clouded eyes.

'I think I've proved my point,' he said quietly.

For a long moment she couldn't speak at all, then the realisation of all that had been happening flooded her veins in a hot, humiliating wave.

'Is that truly what all this was about?' She could barely whisper the words. 'You proving a point?'

The pain was so great she felt faint with it, almost swaying as she stood, trying to make sense of it all. And yet, she realised with a stab of bitter anguish, she could hardly have expected anything else. At the very outset he'd challenged her to prove she didn't want him. She'd accepted the challenge, however foolishly, and she'd failed it. She could hardly blame him if she'd been far more powerfully affected by those devastating kisses than he had.

'I wanted you to face up to the truth,' he said. 'The truth that deep within you there is a passionate woman, though for reasons best known to yourself you seem determined to keep her hidden away.'

Shaken to the core, but clinging to the last vestiges of pride, Clancy pulled herself up to her full height and looked him in the eye, her face drained of colour but resolute.

'If you truly believe you proved your point with that little exhibition, I can only conclude that it is in fact you who is expert in the art of self-deception,' she said with an icy coolness that totally belied the turmoil she was suffering inside. 'And if you really believed my response to you was passionate, I must further assume that, despite all evidence to the contrary, your experience with women has been sadly lacking.'

She took a deep, steadying breath, desperately willing her treacherous body to damp down the last of the fires still smouldering within. 'Now, shall we continue with this walk? I'm beginning to feel rather cold with all this standing about.'

It was a shallow victory at best, but she mentally awarded herself points for effort as she saw the faint but unmistakable glint of anger in his smoke-dark eyes. If nothing else, she thought ruefully, she could congratulate herself for being a terrific actress.

CHAPTER EIGHT

CLANCY was beset by an uncharacteristic attack of nervousness as she got ready to go out to the pub to meet the rest of the team that evening. Glancing over the meagre selection of clothes she'd brought with her and finding nothing remotely suitable for the occasion, she frowned. What on earth was she worrying for? It wasn't a formal event, for goodness' sake, yet here she was dithering about like a schoolgirl preparing for a first date.

With a resigned shrug she turned back to the first outfit she'd tentatively selected, then rejected. The leggings were both casual and comfortable—she'd worn them dozens of times in London without having to think twice about whether they were suitable or not. Now, though, she couldn't help but wonder if they were just a shade too bright, a touch too colourful. Tonight she'd really rather have blended anonymously into the background, but there would be no hope of that in this outfit.

Then she gave a rueful smile—fat chance she'd have of disappearing into the background in any case, since she'd be walking into the pub at Luke's side. She'd be the focus for a dozen sets of curious eyes no matter what she wore.

Rather to her surprise, Luke seemed to like her clothes, judging by the pleased glint in his eyes when he turned up at her door a short while later.

'Very nice,' he murmured approvingly. 'Though with legs as good as yours you hardly need to draw attention to them—they do that on their own.'

If she'd possessed a full-length skirt reaching right to the floor she'd have changed into it there and then.

'I'm not wearing leggings for that reason,' she returned stiffly. 'I simply find them comfortable and easy to wear.'

'Then it's a bonus that they're also easy on the eye,' he countered swiftly. 'Or is that now going to be held as a black mark against them?'

She frowned. 'I don't know what you mean.'

'Don't you?' He eyed her consideringly. 'It seems nowadays that many women go out of their way to conceal their essential femininity. They seem to feel it undermines their quest for equality.'

'Oh, for heaven's sake——' she tossed her head impatiently '—not that old chestnut. I can tell you here and now that I'm perfectly at ease with both my gender and my status in the world—I don't need outward trappings to tell people who and what I am.'

'Really?' Amusement tugged at his mouth as he looked beyond her to the bed in the middle of the room. 'Then why did it apparently take some time to decide just who and what you were going to be this evening?'

Perplexed, she turned to see what he was looking at, belatedly realising she'd left a pile of clothes strewn haphazardly on the bed. She bit her lip—blast the man. He never missed a thing.

'Who and what I am remains constant.' She strove to recover the lost ground. 'What I wear is irrelevant.'

'But, on this occasion at least, particularly fetching.'

Aware that he had, as usual, managed to have the last word, she glowered up at him. Clearly unperturbed, he smiled, and, irritated though she was, she was hard pressed not to smile right back. He had such a devastating smile, she thought helplessly—it seemed to bring light and warmth to the whole room. Turning away before he could wreak any more havoc in her soul, she grabbed a jacket from the chair.

'Let's go,' she said abruptly. 'We don't want to keep your friends waiting.'

The pub was a couple of miles out of town—off the tourist track, Luke informed her as they drove there in his sleek Morgan.

'Since tourists must surely be the life blood of this area, it's a little unfair to malign them, isn't it?' she asked tartly.

He shook his head. 'I'm not maligning them— rather the places which go out of their way to cater to them and couldn't give a damn about the locals.' His features relaxed. 'The place we're going to offers a warm welcome to everyone, tourists and locals alike. It doesn't boost its prices at holiday times or display a range of T-shirts with the pub's name emblazoned on the front. It's just a nice, unassuming little place. You'll see.'

He was right. She felt the warmth of the pub's atmosphere as soon as she walked in the front door—

a warmth that managed to endure even when, as she
predicted, every set of eyes in the place turned to see
who was walking in with Luke. He was clearly a
welcome visitor; that much was obvious from the
smiles and slaps on the back as he made his way to
the bar, Clancy attempting to follow unobtrusively at
his back. Then she realised what she was doing and
mentally gave herself a sharp kick—why should she
be skulking in his shadow, for heaven's sake? She was
a person in her own right, not some trivial little
accessory.

After giving herself a swift pep talk she was able
to square her shoulders and meet the curious glances
with a smile, a smile she was delighted to discover was
returned in full measure.

'So this is the young lady you've been escorting
round the fells.' The barman, a jovial, bearded giant,
chuckled amiably as he winked at Clancy. 'No wonder
you've been keeping her to yourself! Why don't you
come and sit up on one of these bar stools and tell
me all about yourself, little lady? Luke's been mon-
opolising you for quite long enough.'

Luke slid her a querying sideways glance—no doubt
to see how she'd react to the 'little lady' tag, Clancy
realised with amusement. Ordinarily it might well have
rankled, but the playful twinkle in the barman's eye
made it impossible for her to feel even faintly
aggrieved.

'Thank you,' she returned with a twinkle of her
own. 'I believe I will.'

The look of surprise on Luke's face was reward
enough in itself. It was strangely refreshing to realise

she was capable of surprising him—heaven knew, he
did it to her often enough! But her moment of triumph
vanished a second later as the pub door opened and
a stunningly beautiful woman walked in. Tall and
willowy, with a cascade of silver-blonde hair tumbling
over her shoulders, she was quite breathtaking. Clancy
couldn't take her eyes off the girl as she crossed the
floor towards Luke and went straight into his embrace.

'Charlie!' There was no mistaking the pleasure in
his voice as he dropped a light kiss on to her hair. 'I
wasn't sure if you'd be able to make it tonight.'

'When have you ever known me to miss out on a
team spree?' She tapped him playfully on the arm,
her enormous blue eyes laughing up at him. 'Besides
which I was eaten up with curiosity to meet the researcher lady I've heard so much about. Where is
she?'

'I'm right here.' Even though her heart had sunk
right to the bottom of her shoes with the woman's
arrival, Clancy managed to dredge up a polite smile
as she held out her right hand. 'Clancy Hall, at your
service.'

Her heart sank still further as the blonde grasped
her fingers in a pleasantly firm handshake and
smiled warmly. Not only did she look like a goddess,
it seemed she was a genuinely nice person. Was there
no justice in the world? She might at least have had
the decency to be a royal pain, Clancy thought
ruefully.

'Nice to meet you,' she was saying now, her perfectly shaped lips curving into a smile that displayed
flawlessly even white teeth. 'I hear through the

grapevine that Luke's been putting you through a rough time.'

If only she knew the half of it, Clancy reflected wryly as she nodded. 'You could say that.'

'How cruel of you, Luke.' Charlie slid him a teasing look and his returning grin twisted Clancy's heart. He'd never looked at her like that—not once. 'What has the poor girl done to deserve such treatment?'

'Clancy wants to come out with the team on a rescue,' he explained. 'I wanted to make sure she was up to it.'

Clancy opened her mouth to defend herself, then closed it again. Try as she might, she couldn't find fault with his answer. Hard though it was to accept, she knew she should be grateful for his tact. He could quite easily have told this glowing female just what a weakling she'd been when she first arrived.

Charlie nodded gravely. 'It can be very tough in the hills.'

Clancy glanced up interestedly. 'You sound as though you're talking from experience.'

Charlie and Luke exchanged a telling glance, then the blonde shrugged her shoulders dismissively. 'A bit.'

'Never mind "a bit",' Luke retorted swiftly. 'Charlie's a regular member of the team. She's been out on dozens of rescues.'

His words smote Clancy like a hammer-blow, though she managed with a supreme effort not to show it, swallowing hard against the rush of pain. It was all kinds of ridiculous to feel such agonising jealousy, she told herself fiercely—so this golden girl was not only beautiful and nice, she was also courageous and daring. So what?

But even as she remonstrated silently with herself, she knew she wasn't suffering because of Charlie's looks or personality—or even her accomplishments. She was aching deep inside because of the expression in Luke's eyes as he put his arm round Charlie's shoulders and hugged her. It was obvious he was extremely fond of her, and in all honesty Clancy couldn't even find it in her heart to blame him. If she'd been a man she'd probably have been besottedly in love with the beautiful blonde herself. Was he?

The rest of the evening passed in a blur. Outwardly she appeared as normal, chatting and even managing to joke with Charlie and the rest of the team members as they arrived and were introduced. But inwardly— inwardly she was a mess, her emotions running on high as she fought to deny the agonising revelation she'd just experienced.

It was no use, she realised with a helplessness that horrified her. Seeing Luke with Charlie had somehow ripped away the screens from something she'd been desperately trying to hide from herself. Now she was being forced to confront it in all its wonderful and terrible reality. She was in love with Luke MacLennan.

If she had been an actress she'd have deserved an Oscar that evening, Clancy acknowledged painfully some time later. Not by a look, not by a single sign had she betrayed the turmoil crashing about within her like waves on an angry sea. Dan would have known, of course—he'd have taken one glance into her face and seen beyond the smiles and the laughter to the anguish. Just as well he wasn't there—though in many ways she found herself longing for his solid, uncompromising support.

'What sort of research do you do, Clancy?' Charlie materialised beside her at the bar after spending time circulating among her friends.

Clancy shrugged her narrow shoulders. 'Anything and everything really. We've done programmes on a wide range of subjects.'

'You belong to an independent company?' At Clancy's nod, Charlie settled herself on a bar stool, clearly prepared for a chat. 'Are you commissioned to do things, or do you come up with the ideas yourselves?'

'Both.' Clancy spotted Luke across the room, a tiny smile playing about his mouth as he watched the two women together, and a shiver ran over her skin. He must be comparing them, she thought unhappily, and what a picture of contrasts they must make—Charlie so gloriously golden and female, the jeans and sweat-shirt she was wearing doing nothing to conceal her curvaceous figure, and at her side Clancy, small and slight and probably seeming more boyish than ever. For perhaps the first time in her life she found herself wishing she had long legs, a Page Three figure and a tumbling cascade of riotous curls.

'Tell me some of the programmes you've been in-volved with,' Charlie went on, apparently not no-ticing her moment of distraction.

Clancy obligingly reeled off a list of the work the company had done, but stopped short of mentioning the famine documentary. That was still too recent, too raw to be chatted about.

Charlie frowned, her smooth brow creasing in thought. 'I don't believe I've seen any of those.' She made an apologetic little grimace. 'I admit, I'm not a very regular television viewer. Still . . .' she tilted her head to one side as she considered Clancy ' . . . I'm sure I've seen your name on the credits for something.'

Clancy coloured uncomfortably, but made a dismissive little gesture with one hand. 'I'm surprised,' she said, managing to conjure up a light little laugh. 'Most people go and put the kettle on when the credits start to roll.'

Charlie chuckled. 'Which must be somewhat galling for all the hard-working souls who've actually put the piece together. But I've got a friend in the business, so I tend to look out for his name on the screen.'

Spotting the lifeline with a surge of relief, Clancy grabbed at it. 'A friend? What's his name? I might know him.'

As it happened she did vaguely know Charlie's friend, though she'd never actually worked with him, since his line of business ran more to wildlife and nature documentaries. But it gave her something to talk about and an excuse to keep the conversation firmly away from her own work, much to her relief.

They were still chatting some time later when a sudden high noise cut right through the babble of conversation in the pub. Charlie lifted her head, almost like an animal sniffing the air.

'That's Luke's bleeper,' she said tersely. 'The team's being called out.'

Clancy glanced over in Luke's direction. He was already punching numbers into the portable phone he carried everywhere. She couldn't hear what he was saying, but it was clear from the faintly grim expression on his taut features that he was being given details.

'A party of schoolkids,' he announced a moment later as he ended the call. Clancy could only marvel at the way his voice, raised only slightly, instantly silenced the hubbub in the room. 'Went out this morning and haven't returned.'

'Experienced?' Charlie was sliding off the bar stool and reaching for her shoulder-bag as she spoke, her movements fluid and graceful as a cat's.

He shook his head. 'They've hardly got a scrap of equipment between them.'

'Thank heavens it's a mild night at least,' Clancy commented.

Luke shot her an exasperated glance. 'Mild here, perhaps,' he said shortly. 'But up on the hills could be a very different matter.' He looked directly at Charlie. 'Are you OK for another one? You've been out twice in the last few nights.'

She tossed her long blonde hair back over her shoulders with a grin. 'So have you. And you know better than to try stopping me.'

His features relaxed momentarily into a smile, then he looked down at Clancy. 'I'll get one of the others to drive you back to the hotel,' he said. 'We're going straight to the rescue base.'

Stung at such cavalier treatment, she opened her mouth to protest, but bit it back. He had more important things to deal with right now than an offended female, she told herself firmly. Still, she wasn't about to let him send her scuttling home to bed.

'I'll come with you.'

Charlie laid a sympathetic hand on her shoulder. 'Luke's right. You'd be best to go back to the hotel. This wouldn't be a lot of fun for you——'

'Never mind "fun",' Luke cut in impatiently. 'She'd only get in the way.'

Clancy tilted her chin defiantly. 'I thought you were in a hurry to go to the aid of the schoolkids,' she said coolly.

'Oh, for heaven's sake!' It was clear from the expression on his face that he wasn't happy about giving in to her, and even as she stubbornly stood her ground she knew a pang of unhappiness. Where this man was concerned it seemed she had a monopoly on causing aggravation. But she owed it to herself not to be dismissed like a child. 'You can come to the rescue base with us, but no further. All right?'

It was a small victory, but a victory nevertheless, and she wasn't about to cavil, particularly when youngsters were in need of help. She nodded acceptance.

'OK. You go in the van with the others—I'll go ahead with Charlie.'

They headed out towards the car park, Clancy falling in beside the other team members who were clearly too caught up in wondering what lay ahead to show any surprise that she was with them. By the time

they reached the rescue base, Luke had already arrived and changed into mountain gear. Her eyes helplessly drawn to him, she watched in fascination as he
swiftly and calmly, but with complete authority, or-
ganised the team. He was a natural leader, she realised,
born to command and be followed. It was a quality
which must inevitably have emerged, no matter what
career he'd chosen.

It seemed to take mere seconds for the other
members to get ready and clamber into the four-wheel-
drive vehicles parked in the base garage. As she
watched Luke walk towards the lead jeep without so
much as a backward glance, she felt her heart sink in
her chest, even though she knew it was ridiculous. He
was going on a rescue mission—possibly even a
dangerous one. She couldn't in all fairness expect him
to think about her at a time like this.

At the last moment, though, he paused and turned
his head, his searching gaze finding her almost immediately, and she couldn't deny a tiny leap of
gladness.

'If you get tired of waiting, the hotel's only a five-
minute walk from here,' he said. 'We could be gone
for a long time.'

She smiled faintly. 'I'll be here.'

It could only have been a trick of the light or the
shadows, but his eyes seemed to soften. 'I know you
will.' He turned away to climb into the jeep, leaving
her to wonder if she'd imagined or simply misinter-
preted that telling little look. She wasn't given long
to wonder. The vehicles had barely disappeared into
the night when she heard the sound of her own voice

being called, and turned to see the grinning, bearded face of Mark Jones, one of the team she'd driven down with.

'Are you going to stand there wool-gathering all night? Come on, Clancy, we could do with a hand in here.'

'OK.' There was just a faint touch of resignation in her voice. 'Tell me where the kettle is.'

'Kettle?' His fiercely bushy eyebrows shot up to disappear beneath an unruly fringe.

'Well, I assume I'm being put on coffee-making duties?'

He shook his head decisively. 'No time for coffee just now. You're a media type, aren't you?'

She couldn't help but smile at the description. 'Of a sort,' she conceded.

'Great. Then consider yourself Press liaison officer for the duration. It's a job the rest of us hate! Come on, I'll show you where the phones are.'

If she'd harboured any remaining suspicion that she was being fobbed off with a trivial task to keep her occupied and out of harm's way, it was soon to disappear. For the next few hours she seemed never to have a telephone receiver away from her ear as she spoke to reporters from newspapers, television and radio, keeping them all up to date with the progress of the search as information was being relayed back by the team.

'Are the Press always like this when there's a rescue on?' she asked Mark as she laid the phone down on one particularly persistent hack who wouldn't be convinced she didn't yet know the age of the youngest missing child.

'Frequently worse.' He handed her a mug of steaming coffee and perched himself precariously on the desk. 'But when kids are involved it's always newsworthy, and not just to the local media. You've got to remember, too, that this is generally a fairly quiet backwater—we don't have big industrial stories, or lots of crime, thank the lord. What we do have...'

'Is an extremely busy mountain rescue team,' she finished the sentence for him, and he nodded.

'All through the winter you can guarantee we'll be their best source of stories.'

'Must be a nuisance having to deal with them when you're busy,' she commiserated.

He shrugged. 'It can be. Having you here tonight has been a godsend, because it's freed the rest of us up. However, we depend on the Press to publicise us when we're fund-raising, and we're *always* fund-raising! So it's a two-way thing.'

Clancy was silent for a moment, considering her next words carefully. 'I didn't realise the team had been out on rescues recently,' she said at last.

He looked at her in pained surprise. 'Luke hasn't told you?'

She shook her head. 'The first thing I knew about it was when he asked Charlie if she was all right to go out again so soon.'

'Typical Luke.' He gave a wry chuckle, rubbing his bearded chin thoughtfully. 'Typical Charlie too that she'd refuse to be excluded. The two of them probably haven't had more than a dozen hours' sleep in the past week.'

Clancy toyed with the notepad on the desk before her. 'They seem to work well together,' she said casually.

'Luke and Charlie? They're a terrific team—none better. But then it's hardly surprising. They've always been close.'

Clancy nodded, forced to swallow hard against the rush of pain. Well, what had she expected? She'd seen the warmth of their relationship for herself—Mark had simply confirmed what she already knew.

She might have asked more, but the phone began to ring again and she sent him a rueful glance. 'No peace for the wicked. This time they'll probably ask me what colour socks the kids are wearing.'

'You're learning fast!'

Busy as she was, it was still the longest night Clancy could ever remember experiencing, made longer still by the increasingly worried looks on the faces of the base back-up crew. As Luke had predicted, conditions on the hills were far from hospitable. Fresh snow had fallen since the school party had made its way up there, effectively obliterating most of the tracks, and Luke had reported back that temperatures were well below freezing.

'We'll be looking at cases of hypothermia at least,' Mark said grimly. 'We can only pray they've had enough sense to seek shelter—and that they haven't gone to sleep, because that's when the body temperature falls even faster.'

As the long, never-ending night continued, Clancy began almost to feel like two people—one part of her dealing capably and efficiently with the many Press enquiries coming in—the other somewhere out on the dark and icy fells with Luke. In a strange and totally inexplicable way, she felt closer to him than she'd ever been, as though she was somehow managing to tune in to his thoughts.

That realisation shook her to the core—she'd grown accustomed to that sort of psychic link with Dan; heaven knew, they'd been sharing one another's thoughts since they were in the cradle. But it had never happened with another living soul. She shook her head irritably. She was imagining things; she must be. It was simply the effect of this long, traumatic night. It couldn't possibly be anything else.

Washed over by a sudden wave of weariness, she rested her forehead against her steepled hands, closing her eyes for a brief moment.

'Where are you, Luke?' she whispered. 'Are you safe?'

She could see his face in her mind's eye—that stern, uncompromising face that could devastate her with its rare illuminating smile. He seemed to be searching the far horizon, his smoky grey eyes sweeping the land. There was tiredness in those eyes, an exhaustion that only sheer determination was keeping at bay.

'Hang on in there, Luke,' she murmured softly. 'You can make it. The kids are depending on you.'

She never knew how long she sat there, silently sending her message of strength, but the mood was suddenly shattered as a great cheer went up from the team members clustered round the radio equipment.

'They've been found!' Mark rushed to her side, gripping her shoulders in his excitement. 'The kids—they've been found!'

'Are they OK?'

He nodded, his eyes dancing triumphantly. 'Cold, shaken and half-starved, Charlie says, but otherwise unhurt.' He nodded towards the telephone, which had been uncharacteristically quiet for a while. 'Get ready, kid,' he said jubilantly. 'That thing's about to turn red-hot.'

CHAPTER NINE

CLANCY didn't see the youngsters when they were brought back to safety that night. Mindful of the Press corps hovering like hungry flies at the rescue base, Mark had arranged for ambulances to be waiting to pick the children and their teachers up at the foot of the fells.

'Charlie says none of them has suffered any actual injury,' he reported to the others. 'But it's always as well to get them thoroughly checked over in hospital. In all likelihood they'll only be kept in overnight.' He glanced at his watch with a rueful grin. 'What's left of overnight, that is!'

The late grey dawn of a winter's morning was indeed beginning to break when the Land Rovers bearing the mountain rescue team finally made it back to base. Clancy stood with the others, feeling strangely shy as she watched Luke clamber down from the jeep.

'What is this?' he said, a smile lighting his tired eyes. 'A welcoming party?'

'Sounds to me as though you deserve one, man.' Mark strode forward and grasped Luke's hand in a firm handshake. 'Twelve kids and two teachers returned safe and sound. A lot of families will be sleeping more easily tonight.'

Luke nodded, but he was looking over Mark's shoulder. When he spotted Clancy his eyes grew stern. 'I thought I told you to go home,' he rasped.

'And I told you I'd still be here.' Gripped by a longing that was all but overwhelming to simply fling herself into his arms, she stood rooted to the spot, afraid to move.

'She's been terrific, Luke,' Mark cut in. 'She's kept the Press off our backs all night. She can join the team any time she likes.'

Luke's expression was unreadable as he walked over to her and she gripped her hands into tight fists at her sides, still afraid they'd disobey the commands of her brain and simply reach out to touch him.

'So you did well,' he said.

After the long night when she'd felt so emotionally in tune with him, it was nearly more than she could bear to now be so physically close to him and yet be unable to do anything about it. She barely dared even look at him in case he'd see the longing that must be written in her eyes. With a supreme effort she managed to shrug dismissively.

'I didn't do very much. You and Charlie and the others are the real heroes of the night.'

To her astonishment, he reached out and gently stroked a wayward strand of hair back from her forehead, and she shivered beneath his feather-light touch.

'Don't put yourself down,' he said softly. 'The support of the back-up crew was invaluable.'

For long moments she could only gaze at him, lost in the depths of his eyes, unable to move away from the warmth of his fingers on her cheek.

'Wh—uh—where's Charlie?' she managed to stutter at last.

'Gone home. We dropped her off on the way back.' His features took on a mock-stern expression as he wagged a finger under her nose. 'And that, young lady, is where you're going too. Home to bed.'

'What about you?' she countered, relieved beyond measure to have a reason to return to a faintly waspish tone. If she'd looked much longer into those incredible eyes, she'd have been in real danger of dissolving. 'I reckon you need to be in bed just as much as I do.'

She wasn't even aware of the innuendo in her own words until a dangerously teasing grin curved his mouth.

'Is that an invitation?'

A sudden unbidden vision came into her mind of lying in his arms, pressed close against his powerful body, naked skin against naked skin, and the swift retort she'd been framing died unspoken on her lips.

'Certainly not,' she managed to sputter indignantly at last, horribly aware that a scarlet heat was flooding her skin. 'What do you think I am?'

'What do I think you are?' He pondered the question for a moment, then shook his head. 'Ah, no, Clancy, that's something that will have to wait for another time, a time when we can talk and listen—a time when we're not both out on our feet. Come on—I'll drive you back to the hotel.'

'You don't have to,' she said quickly, not at all sure she could cope with the strain of being alone with Luke in the intimate confines of his Morgan, even for the few short minutes it would take to reach the hotel. 'I'm sure Mark or one of the others could take me back. Or I could walk—it's not far. Maybe the fresh air might even do me some good . . . help me unwind enough to get to sleep. I've never found it easy to sleep in daylight, even when I am tired.'

Hearing her own voice begin to babble, she let it trail away. It was because she was tired, she rationalised silently. Heaven knew, it was tough enough being alone with him at any time, but right now all her defences were in real danger of crumbling clean away, leaving her vulnerable not only to him, but to herself and the clamouring demands of her own body.

'Are you quite finished?' he asked now, having waited patiently throughout the monologue. 'Then go and get your bag, I'm taking you home.'

Tiredness had a lot to answer for, she thought ruefully as she went to collect her things. In any normal circumstances she'd have downright refused to be bossed about by a man—yet here she was, trotting off to do his bidding like an obedient little girl. Dan would never believe it. Then she gave a little snort of self-disgust. Who was she trying to kid? Tiredness had precious little to do with it. The truth of the matter was, Luke MacLennan was a strong man and a forceful personality—and, however else she might feel about him, she couldn't deny having an enormous respect, maybe even admiration for him.

All the more reason that she should be standing up for herself against him, she told herself irritably as she snatched up her jacket and bag from the chair she'd carelessly flung them on to so many hours ago. If she weren't extremely careful she'd be no better than all those other women who followed his every move with sheep-like adoration.

They drove back to the hotel in silence, Clancy doing her utmost to keep as far away from him as was possible in the vehicle. It made no difference. Every nerve-ending she possessed seemed to be quivering on the very surface of her skin. She gazed sightlessly out of the window as they drove through the empty streets—what on earth was happening to her? He'd made no move to touch her or even to look at her since she'd slid into the passenger seat beside him, yet her entire being was focused solely on him.

She'd expected him to simply drop her off at the hotel, but to her surprise he drove into the car park and switched off the engine.

'This is just fine,' she said hastily. 'I can manage perfectly well from here.'

He slid her an ironic sideways grin. 'It's all right, I wouldn't attempt to demean your liberated status by doing anything as chauvinistic as accompanying you to the door.' His grey eyes were faintly challenging as he turned his head to look at her. 'But I was hoping you might be kind enough to offer me a cup of coffee.'

'Coffee?' She stared at him with wide, suspicious eyes. 'Can't you make one for yourself back at your own home?' Since she and Dan had been brought up from an early age to be hospitable, it went against the grain to be so ungracious, but the prospect of having him in her room right now was definitely more than she could hope to cope with.

'I could,' he returned gravely, 'but I'm not going home. I'm going to the office to write up a report on the night first.'

'You're *what*?' Indignation that he should be so cavalier about his welfare drove caution for her own state of health straight out of the window. 'Don't be ridiculous, Luke—you need sleep, and a lot of it by the look of you. You're exhausted.'

'Then make me a cup of coffee. That'll keep me going for a little while longer.'

'For heaven's sake!' Infuriated by his intransigence, she tore off the seatbelt and clambered out of the car, scowling darkly at him as he joined her. 'Don't you have any sense at all? Don't you know what you can do to yourself if you don't get enough sleep?' She was still berating him, albeit in a lowered voice, as they entered the hotel and headed towards the stairs. He took it all in silence, an amused glint playing in his eyes, until they reached her room.

'Are you quite finished?' he asked mildly as she closed the door behind them.

'I've barely begun.' She planted both hands on her hips, her lips pressed tightly together as she glowered up at him.

'Then I suggest you save the rest for later.'

'Oh, do you, indeed? Well I . . .' Whatever she was about to say disappeared in a muffled squawk of outrage as he calmly hooked one arm beneath her knees and lifted her clean off her feet, as easily as if she'd been made of feathers.

'Just what do you think you're doing?' Since being in his arms had sent a jolt of sheer undiluted joy charging through her entire body, it was hard to manufacture indignation, but she did her best.

He grinned unrepentantly as he crossed the room in a couple of strides and tossed her on to the bed. 'There's no "think" about it,' he answered solemnly. 'I know exactly what I'm doing—and you've only yourself to blame.'

'I have?' Before her astonished eyes he shrugged off the thermal jacket he'd been wearing and began unbuttoning the thick plaid shirt.

He nodded. 'There's only one surefire way I know of to shut up a badgering woman.'

As the shirt and several other layers of winter mountain gear joined the jacket in a heap on the floor, she began to edge her way to the side of the bed nearest the door.

'If you're planning an escape, I wouldn't bother,' he continued relentlessly. 'Unless you wouldn't mind being pursued along hotel corridors by a naked mountaineer, that is.'

The very idea made her close her eyes in horror. Then she opened them again, glaring at him accusingly. 'You've come up here under entirely false pretences! You said you wanted coffee, to help you stay awake.'

Dressed now only in breeches, he dropped down on to the bed beside her and she swallowed hard, her eyes helplessly riveted to his magnificent chest with its lavish black silky pelt just crying out to be touched.

'So I did,' he returned solemnly, with just the faintest trace of mockery. 'But I've thought of a better way to stave off sleep.'

She could only watch in helpless fascination as he slowly reached out, her eyes unable to leave his as he gently but firmly clasped her arm and pulled her towards him.

'Luke, this is crazy,' she murmured brokenly. 'We can't do this.'

'Can't we?' His arms closed about her, his lips whispering into her hair. 'Tell me why, Clancy.'

'Because it's wrong.' She tried to twist away, but the movement only brought her face against his shoulder, and the warm, masculine scent of his naked skin flooded her veins. Unable to help herself, she pressed her lips to his throat as his hand came up to cup the back of her head.

'What could possibly be wrong in two people finding comfort and joy in each other's arms?'

But what about love? The anguished question rang in her mind and she looked up at him with stricken eyes, half afraid he might have heard the words. Then her eyes fluttered helplessly closed as he tilted her chin with his fingers, bringing her mouth round to meet his, and any hope she might still have had of fighting him vanished with the sweet warmth of his kiss.

His mouth moved over hers, gently at first, his caress a feather-light exploration. Her lips parted, hungry for more of him, thirsting for the honeyed taste of him. Her hands moved restlessly to his chest,

unable to resist the lure of the silky dark hair, her
fingers pressing through the warm skin below. Where
her hands had touched, the rest of her body ached to
touch also, and when he pulled the sweatshirt over
her head, tossing it carelessly to the floor, she was
happy to let him, immediately wriggling back into his
embrace, unable to stifle a groan of sheer pleasure as
her naked breasts pushed against his chest. All thought
of resistance was gone. Nothing mattered any more
but the man holding her so possessively, his lips and
hands roaming freely over her heated skin. All reality
was centred in him—and as her mind gladly relin-
quished control she gloried in its surrender.

Somehow he'd shed his few remaining clothes,
somehow he'd stripped the skin-tight leggings from
her, almost without her even noticing they'd gone, so
caught up was she in the whirlwind of passion he'd
created in her blood.

'What do you want me to do, Clancy?'

Her eyes flew open, gazing up at him in clouded
confusion as he pressed her back against the bed, his
body a welcome weight on top of hers. He smiled tenderly, dropping a kiss on to the corner of her mouth.

'I won't make love to you unless you tell me you
want me, Clancy. I'd never force you.'

Somewhere in the depths of her mind a tiny sane
voice cried that she should stop him now, while she
still could—a voice that told her she could never be
the same again if she made love with him now. But
other voices came, clamouring, insistent voices telling
her she was already in way too deep, that if she pushed
him away now she'd spend the rest of her life won-

dering what it would have been like to share the beauty of his love. Even if it was for just a single night.

'Make love to me, Luke,' she murmured softly. 'I want you.'

As if to seal some unspoken pledge, he kissed her, his mouth warm and gentle on hers.

'Don't worry, little one,' he said with a tenderness that threatened to bring tears to her eyes. 'I'll look after you.' He turned away from her for a moment and she felt the loss as acutely as if a part of her own body had been wrenched away. When he came back into her arms she welcomed him gladly, made whole again by his embrace. His hand slipped down to stroke the soft skin of her thighs and she whimpered her need for him, opening up to his questing fingers like a dew-wet flower. She was caught up in something she'd never experienced before, could never even have imagined before Luke—a storm in her blood both wild and beautiful, a wild tempest of longing that he and he alone could satisfy.

Even as he slid deep inside her, the tiny part of her brain that was still capable of conscious thought knew she'd never get over this experience. It wasn't just making love—somehow this far transcended a mere physical joining of bodies. No other man would ever be able to touch her as deeply or stir her as profoundly as he was doing now. No other man would ever be able to call to her soul with his caresses. No matter what happened after tonight, he was a part of her now, a part that could never be erased.

Then thought stilled as he moved within her, and, untutored though she was in the act of love, she began

moving with him, her body instinctively finding its
own rhythms in tune with his. Driven by some inner
force, she arched up against him, trying to take him
deeper and deeper still into the very heart of her, until
the pounding beat of need building up within her grew
to a very crescendo. Unknowing, she cried his name
aloud, instinctively clutching to him as she was flung
heedlessly into a beautiful unknown place.

When reality slowly returned she opened her eyes,
half afraid of what she would see in his. But instead
of the cool masculine triumph she'd feared she saw
only a soft light.

'Are you OK?' he murmured.

She nodded, not at all sure she could even find a
voice to answer him in words.

'We have to talk, Clancy. But not now.' He rolled
over on to his back, his arms still holding her with a
sweet possessiveness that went straight to her heart.
'Now we have to rest.' Even as he spoke his dark lashes
were lowering over his eyes and within seconds he was
asleep, his breathing slow and rhythmic. But even
though she was exhausted she couldn't bring herself
to give in to unconsciousness, couldn't bear to let go
of the moment.

She wasn't a fool. Even now, with her body still
feeling the tingling warmth of the passion they'd
shared, she knew that, however incredible the experience had been for her, for him it could have been
no more than another sweet night in a long line of
them. He wanted to talk—doubtless to let her down
gently, to say she shouldn't expect anything more than
he'd already given. Perhaps he'd tell her that it had

been a mistake—that he'd turned to her because Charlie hadn't been there for him.

She could cope. Even though her heart dulled within her like a leaden weight at the thought of losing him now, she could cope. In a strange way, she felt she owed that to him. Lying here now, even with the knowledge of all that must inevitably come, she felt at peace with herself, perhaps more at peace than she'd ever known. He'd given her that—now it was up to her to thank him by letting go. Or at least by convincing him she could let go. She hadn't meant to sleep, had wanted to stay awake savouring the moments of lying close to him, feeling his skin against her skin, the steady beat of his heart beneath her cheek. If this was all she was ever going to have of him, she wanted to hoard each precious moment like a miser with his gold. But sleep wouldn't be foiled and eventually she succumbed to its insistent demands, her eyes refusing to stay open a second longer.

When she finally woke, she was aware of a sense of loss even before she opened her eyes, and it was with a sense of dull inevitability that she realised Luke was no longer at her side. Well, what had she expected, she asked herself viciously, deliberately turning her pain against herself, another passionate love-making session? A cosily intimate brunch for two? It was better this way, she decided resolutely, better to be swift and brutal. Drawing things out could only prolong the inevitable agony.

She was in the shower when the telephone rang, standing immobile beneath the jets of water as though they could somehow wash away the memory of the

night. Moving slowly, she shrugged her shoulders into
a towelling robe, hesitating before she picked up the
receiver. If it was Luke calling, she wasn't ready to
talk to him yet—hadn't soldered on the armour she'd
need to face him.

'Hello?'

'Clancy? Don't tell me you're still in bed? It's the
middle of the afternoon, girl!'

'Dan?' Relief that it wasn't Luke made her light-
headed. 'Are you calling from the office?'

'Not exactly.' His voice was lightly teasing. 'I'm
downstairs.'

'Here? In the hotel—but why?'

'Come on down and I'll tell you all about it. Or
else I'll come up there.'

She glanced at the rumpled bed and shook her head
hastily. Dan would spot that right away—and she
wasn't up to facing a brotherly interrogation right
now.

'Just give me a couple of minutes to fling on some
clothes. I'll meet you downstairs.'

He was waiting for her in the foyer, and she felt a
rush of real gladness as she went straight into his out-
stretched arms. He'd always been a rock for her, the
one person she knew who would always give his un-
questioning love and support. Well, perhaps not un-
questioning, she amended wryly as she pulled back to
look into his warm eyes.

'You look great!' he said. 'There's colour in your
cheeks—and I think you've even put on a bit of
weight. Much needed it was, too. What have you been
doing with yourself?'

'Never mind that now. Just give me another hug.'

His arms went round her again, holding her so tightly she could barely breathe, and she closed her eyes, laying her head on his shoulder.

'Oh, Dan,' she murmured. 'It's so good to see you. I've really missed you.' Then she raised her head, only to look straight over his shoulder into a pair of ice-cool grey eyes.

'Luke!' Flustered by his unexpected arrival on the scene, she felt herself colouring vividly. 'I'd like you to meet Dan, my partner and my——'

'Dan.' His voice, curt and clipped, sliced through her introduction and she blinked in surprise. Whatever else she could have said about Luke, she'd never have accused him of being unmannerly. Dan appeared not to have noticed, his face lighting up with his usual boyish grin as he held out his right hand.

'So you're Luke MacLennan,' he said warmly. 'I've heard a great deal about you.'

Luke took his proffered hand but his expression remained grim. 'Really? Clancy's told me nothing about you.'

'Luke!'

If he even heard the remonstrance in her voice he chose to ignore it, turning his head only slightly to address her. 'I'm going to the pool. I'll expect you there in ten minutes.'

'The pool?' Sheer astonishment sent her eyebrows shooting upwards. 'But aren't you exhausted?'

His lips twisted mockingly. 'Is there any reason why I should be?'

Not waiting for her reply, he strode away, his long legs carrying him across the foyer as Clancy stood in stunned silence.

'Phew!' Dan pretended to wipe his brow. 'So that's the dynamic, enigmatic etc. etc. Luke MacLennan. You omitted to mention he's also a man of steel—or maybe rock would be more appropriate.' He grinned down at her. 'Is he always so welcoming?'

Utterly perplexed, Clancy shook her head. 'I've never heard him be so abrupt with anyone. Not even me.'

Dan shrugged philosophically. 'He obviously wasn't bowled over instantly by my charm. It happens.' He put his arm round Clancy's shoulder and gave her a friendly squeeze. 'What about you—have you managed against admittedly considerable odds to resist his charms?'

She might have been able to lie if the question had been asked by anyone else. But Dan knew her too well—one glimpse into her hazel eyes would be enough to tell him everything he wanted to know. And she couldn't keep her eyes averted forever. Accepting the inevitable, she heaved a resigned sigh.

'As a matter of fact—no, I haven't.'

'I knew it!' he crowed delightedly. 'I knew it wasn't just the Lake District that was putting such a bloom in your cheeks.' Then he frowned. 'But how does he feel about you, Clance? If he's giving you a hard time, so help me I'll . . .'

Smiling, she pressed her fingers to his mouth. 'You'll what—sort him out? Not this time, brother darling. This time you're going to have to let me fight my battles all alone.'

'So it is a battle?' His features hardened. 'Just let me at him, the swine. I don't care if he is twelve feet tall and built like a tree.'

She couldn't help but laugh, both amused and touched by his defence. 'It's all right, Dan, really. In any case, I'm not so sure whether the battle's really with him—or with myself.'

He rolled his eyes heavenwards. 'Like that, is it? Then you're right, there really isn't anything I can do. This time you're on your own, kiddo.'

She nodded. 'Don't I know it! Still . . .' she sent him her brightest, most patently false smile '. . . he's a good central figure for the documentary, don't you think?'

It was an old ploy, but a successful one. She'd always been able to distract Dan by turning his attention to his work, which was his greatest and most enduring passion. He immediately started describing ideas he'd had for the mountain rescue programme, the words tumbling over one another in his enthusiasm. Then he stopped abruptly.

'Hey, I shouldn't be going on like this. Aren't you meant to be meeting Luke at the pool?'

'He thinks so.' She jutted her chin defiantly. 'But I'm not at his beck and call, and anyway I've got more important things to do—like chat with you.'

Dan looked distinctly dubious. 'Are you sure? I'm not about to disappear anywhere. But your Luke MacLennan doesn't strike me as the kind of man you can play games with and live to tell the tale.'

'He is not *my* Luke MacLennan,' she countered swiftly, even though the denial cut her to the heart. In a bid to cover the moment of pain, she angled a teasing grin at him. 'What's the matter—scared he'll chase you out of town because I prefer your company to his?'

'Chasing me out of town would probably be the kindest thing he'd think of doing to me,' Dan retorted. 'Look, let's reach a compromise here. I quite fancy a dip myself, and I've brought trunks with me. Let's both go to the pool.'

She hesitated, but only for a moment. Dan was right, it was a reasonable compromise, and in any case a tiny part of her couldn't resist the thought of showing off her new-found confidence in the water to her twin.

'OK,' she said. 'Meet you there in five.'

'Make it three,' he begged solemnly. 'I've got a lot of ground to make up with your...' Seeing the warning glint in her eye, he held up one hand. 'Sorry, with absolutely positively definitely *not* your Luke MacLennan.'

Luke was already swimming when they reached the pool, his muscular body slicing through the water, and despite herself Clancy couldn't help a twist of longing as she watched him. How could she feel anything else? she wondered helplessly, knowing the very sight of this man would always be enough to make her entire being quiver with joy.

Reaching the side of the pool, he spotted Clancy, his eyes narrowing as he saw Dan at her side.

'Are you going to stand there all day?' he barked harshly, and her smile of greeting died on her lips. She hadn't known exactly what to expect after their night together, but it certainly hadn't been this icy coldness. Could he really regret being with her so savagely?

Stung by his unfairness, she glowered darkly back at him. 'I was just about to get in,' she said stiffly. 'There's no need to be so overbearing.'

She ignored Dan's sharp intake of breath, barely noticed the restraining hand he laid on her arm, too incensed by Luke's arrogance to even care that interested eyes were watching from all around the pool.

Luke's lips thinned to a narrow line—the same lips that had pressed against her own with such sensual warmth just a few short hours ago. 'I didn't intend to be overbearing,' he said with unconcealed impatience. 'But I don't have time to waste today.'

'Then don't waste any of it,' she snapped, the words torn from her before she could do anything about it. 'I can manage perfectly well in the pool now.'

He raised one scornful eyebrow. 'Having watched you come close to drowning, forgive me if I don't share your confidence.'

Colouring faintly at the memory of that first abortive swim, she tossed her head dismissively. 'Things have changed since then,' she said shortly. 'And, in any case, Dan's here today.'

At her side Dan gave a barely stifled curse. 'Gee, thanks, kid,' he muttered through clenched teeth. 'That'll really put me high up on his Christmas card list!' But he summoned up his brightest smile to beam amiably down at Luke. 'Yes, indeed, don't you worry about Clancy. She'll be just fine with me.' He slid her a look from beneath his eyelashes. 'If I don't wring her neck, that is,' he said in a voice intended only for her.

'Very well.' In one easy, athletic move, Luke pulled himself from the water. 'I'll leave you to it——'

'I'd like to talk to you later,' Dan cut in hastily. 'To fix up times and locations for a preliminary shoot.'

Luke nodded. 'Tomorrow morning. In my office.' Then he strode off without another word, leaving Dan and Clancy to exchange faintly sheepish looks.

'Why does he make me feel like a wayward child?' Dan complained.

'Probably because you *are* a wayward child.' Deep inside a cold, hard lump of unmitigated misery had settled in the pit of Clancy's stomach, but not for worlds would she have allowed it to show. Managing to dredge up a reasonably authentic-sounding giggle from somewhere, she gave Dan a playful shove, hard enough to topple him off-balance. But her own laughter turned into a shriek as he grabbed her arms to save himself, successfully taking her with him as he fell into the water with a resounding splash.

She was only submerged for a matter of seconds before she managed to resurface, her eyes dancing in playful vengeance as she made a lunge for Dan. 'You great idiot! You didn't have to pull me in too.'

'It's your own fault for shoving me in the first place!'

Taking a deep breath, she plunged back beneath the water, making a grab for his legs, and for a few moments they really were like children, playing and cavorting like young seals. At last, breathless from the exertion, Dan grabbed her by the shoulders as they both trod water, his eyes gazing at her incredulously.

'Good grief, Clancy, is this really you? I've never even been able to lure you out of the shallows before, yet here you are doing a fair impersonation of a mermaid. Is this all Luke's doing?'

She tried to shrug it off, but her eyes told him everything he wanted to know, and he pursed his mouth in a silent whistle of appreciation. 'The more I hear, the more I stand in awe of him,' he said. 'Clark Kent, move over—your career as Superman appears to be under severe threat.'

'Don't be so ridic...' But the words blocked in her throat as she glanced towards the edge of the pool and saw Luke still standing there. He must have been watching all the time, she realised. Yet there was no amusement in his expression, no pride at the sight of his previously terrified pupil enjoying herself in the water. In his eyes she saw only anger. Cold, hard, uncompromising anger.

CHAPTER TEN

CLANCY didn't see Luke for the rest of the day. She kept trying to convince herself she was pleased about that, after the foul mood he'd been in. It wasn't true. Much as it pained her to admit it, she missed him, finding no substitute even in Dan's easygoing company. By the time she went to bed her earlier irritation had simmered itself into a thoroughly bad mood, bringing with it a thumping headache. The pain in her temples she was able to write off to tiredness. The mood wasn't so easily explained.

'You're in a stinker just because you haven't seen him all day,' she told her own reflection morosely as she stared into the mirror, wondering what had happened to the bloom in her cheeks Dan had complimented her on so whole-heartedly. 'That's the long and the short of it.'

Well, she'd have to start getting used to not having him around. Now that Dan was here, her part in the project was all but complete. Tomorrow she'd show him round the places Luke had taken her to, and if possible introduce him to some of the other team members. After that—the programme was in his hands. She'd head back to London and start another piece of research. Except of course that Dan would probably want her to be with the crew for the shoot itself, as she usually was.

The very idea made her shudder. It would be hard enough tearing herself away once—she couldn't come back for more, couldn't put herself through the mill all over again, just to say goodbye at the end of it all.

It would help matters considerably if she could find some pleasure in the thought of going back to London, she thought sadly. Almost without her re-alising it, the Lake District had laid claim to part of her soul, its wild, untamed beauty affecting her in a way no other place ever had. The very thought of busy city streets and pavements crowded with anonymous faces was suffocating.

But Luke must never know that. Her features set in grim, determined lines as she made the silent pledge. For the sake of her own pride, she'd somehow con-vince him she couldn't wait to get back to the capital, back to a very different way of life.

She slept fitfully that night, her rest troubled by dreams of snow-covered mountains and dark, angry eyes, but somewhere in the long hours her subcon-scious must have reached a decision, a decision she blurted out to Dan as soon as she joined him for breakfast.

'I'm going home today.'

'You're what?' He all but choked on a mouthful of coffee, his eyes wide in surprise. 'Don't be crazy—I need you as a guide.'

'Luke can take you anywhere you want to go—or one of the other team members will. You'll probably get further without me anyway, since he still hasn't considered me fit enough for a full-scale recce.'

Dan frowned. 'What's all this about, Clance? What's the sudden rush?'

She hesitated before answering, knowing she'd never be able to convince him with a lie. If she said she was hankering to get back to the city, he'd see through it straight away. He knew perfectly well she'd never been fully at home in London, had only settled there because it was the best base for the company.

'Because I need to get away from here,' she said at last.

He gave a disgusted snort. 'Away from Luke, you mean.'

'Perhaps.' Deliberately schooling her features to remain expressionless, she reached for the coffee-pot. 'But, in any case, you don't really need me here. You'll probably get on a lot better with Luke if I'm not around.'

'So you're just going to cut and run?' He shook his head in pained disbelief. 'I've never known you to do that, Clancy. Not even on the famine shoot.'

'Well, I'm doing it now,' she returned with a calmness that was totally at odds with the way she was really feeling inside.

'I won't allow it.'

In different circumstances she'd probably have laughed at the very idea of Dan trying to put his foot down, but the grimness in his eyes left no room for amusement. Painfully aware that they were having the first real showdown of their lives, she laid a hand over his.

'Please don't give me a hard time over this, Dan,' she appealed to him. 'It's best this way—take my word for it.'

'Damnation!' Unable to resist her plea, it was the only way he could vent his frustration. 'This is all his fault, isn't it?'

'His fault, my fault—what does it matter?' She smiled tenderly, understanding his anger. 'I just know I need to get away.' She gazed into his eyes, squeezing his hand in her own as she silently asked for his acceptance.

'Good morning.'

Clancy jumped as though she'd been shot, Luke's unheralded arrival taking her completely by surprise. She looked up, her heart sinking as she saw the same forbidding expression he'd been wearing the day before.

'Won't you sit down and join us for coffee?' Ever affable, Dan went to pull out a chair, but Luke shook his head.

'I think not.' He glanced pointedly downwards and Clancy belatedly realised she was still holding Dan's hand, though perhaps it would have been more accurate to say she was clinging to it for dear life, her knuckles white with the pressure she was exerting. 'I didn't intend to interrupt an intimate moment.'

Intimate? Clancy's smooth brow furrowed in puzzlement at his choice of word, but before she could say anything Luke was speaking again.

'I'm afraid I shall be busy all morning,' he said, addressing himself to Dan as if she weren't even there.

'However, I can see you in my office this afternoon. Clancy will give you directions.'

Which was a subtle but unmistakable way of saying she wasn't invited along, Clancy acknowledged silently, as she reached for a slice of toast she didn't want and gave all her attention to spreading it with butter. She'd been on the verge of telling Luke she intended to leave that morning, but now she bit the words back, afraid she couldn't trust her own voice to remain steady.

'Very well, Luke.' For reasons she couldn't begin to fathom, there was just the slightest trace of amusement in Dan's voice and she glanced at him in astonishment. His sense of humour had always been a shade off the wall, it was true, but what on earth could he possibly be finding funny in this? 'I'll come along after lunchtime. If I can drag myself away from Clancy, that is.'

Luke's lips tightened perceptibly, but he made no further comment other than to give a single abrupt nod before turning on his heel and stalking away across the dining-room.

'What in the name of all things wonderful was that all about?' Clancy's hazel eyes turned piercingly on Dan. 'What kind of a game are you playing?'

He gave a tiny shrug. 'Since you're in so much of a rush to get away, you'll never know.'

'Dan!' Her voice rose threateningly, but he simply grinned.

'I'll do a deal with you, Clance. Stay till I've seen Luke. Come out for a quick walk on the fells with me this morning and help me acclimatise a bit before

I submit myself to the none too tender mercies of the mountain king. Then we can have a talk this evening, get a few basic plans of action sorted out. You can leave tomorrow morning in clear conscience then.'

'My conscience is perfectly clear,' she muttered ungraciously. 'But if it's that important to you, I'll stay.'

'Good girl.'

They walked for some time in silence, Clancy content to simply drink in the sights and sounds of the countryside she'd come to love so much in such a short time, knowing with an infinite sadness that she might never see it again. Except in dreams. She'd never be able to come here again while Luke was still around— yet it was his presence, a presence she could feel even now, that made the place so special. Without him it would still be mesmerisingly beautiful, but it would no longer have that unique hold on her heart. Face it kid, she told herself silently, if he were at your side even the most desolate landscape would seem beautiful.

'Hey, can we stop and rest for a minute?' Red in the face and out of breath, Dan grabbed her arm to slow her steps.

'What's wrong, brother dear?' she returned with heartless amusement. 'Not up to it?'

'Not used to it,' he admitted. 'My lungs are obviously too full of London smog to cope with all this fresh air. You're doing well, though,' he said admiringly. 'We must have covered a fair distance, yet you still seem as fresh as a daisy.'

'I've been working hard to get fit. You'll have to
do the same thing if you seriously intend to feature
a real rescue in the documentary. The team won't hang
back waiting for you.'

He nodded. 'I know. I'll take the Luke MacLennan
get-fit course before we start. It's obviously worked
wonders for you.' He glanced at his wristwatch and
pursed his lips. 'And, speaking of Mr MacLennan,
I'd better start heading back, or I'll be late for our
appointment. It wouldn't do to keep the great man
waiting. Are you coming with me or do you want to
stay out a while longer?'

Clancy hesitated, torn between the clearly sensible
option of returning to the village and a strange but
intense longing to stay among the hills for just a little
while longer. If this truly was all she would ever have
of the Lake District fells, she wanted to make the most
of each precious second.

'Would you be able to find your own way back?'
she asked doubtfully.

He nodded. 'Sure. We stuck to the path all the way
here, didn't we?'

'OK.' She allowed herself to be convinced. 'Then
I'll stay up here a little while longer.'

'Don't make it too long.' He touched her cheek with
a gentle hand. 'I wouldn't want to have to send the
rescue team out looking for you.'

She rolled her eyes in mock-horror. 'Heaven forbid!'

She watched him as he walked away, then picked
up her rucksack. She wouldn't go very much further,
she decided—just to the crest of the next slope, just
far enough to savour what she felt sure must be a

wonderful view. Then, since she hadn't brought a
camera along, she'd tuck all the memories deep into
her mind to be brought out and enjoyed at some later
date when the pain had mellowed. If that glorious
day ever came.

She was deep in thought as she walked, barely no-
ticing how far she was travelling, her footsteps sure
and steady on the path. Dan had been right, she
realised with a sense of wonder—she really was much
fitter than she had been when she first arrived. And
she could only thank one person for that.

It was a shame in a way that all his efforts would
have been for nothing, since she was quitting before
going on the rescue mission he'd been making her
fitten up for. But enough was enough. She couldn't
deliberately put herself through any more angst over
Luke. Seeing the cold, contemptuous anger in his eyes
only hours after he'd transported her to the stars with
his lovemaking had been devastating. And that anger
could only have been there because he felt guilty over
being unfaithful to Charlie. If she stayed any longer,
that anger could turn even to hate, and she could never
bear that.

With a sigh she dragged herself up the last few steps
to the top of the slope, then stood transfixed in wide-
eyed horror. She'd been expecting to see a glorious
vista of lakes and fells spread out all around her.
Instead, all she could see was a thick, unrelenting
blanket of grey fog. For a moment she could only
gaze downwards in total astonishment, then a cold
hand seemed to close over her heart as she realised
that the swirling mists were moving higher.

Galvanised into sudden action, she hefted the
rucksack into a more comfortable spot on her back
and turned swiftly to retrace her steps. But bare seconds had passed before she was enveloped in the
cloud, a dense, malevolent mass that completely dis-
orientated her. Feeling the first stirrings of panic, she
forced herself to stand still as she vainly tried to get
her bearings.

'It must be this way,' she muttered. 'So long as I'm
heading downhill and straight ahead, I must be going
in the right direction.' She searched in her mind for
any words of advice Luke might have given her on
how best to deal with fog, but came up with nothing.
A rueful little smile touched her lips—she knew how
to use an ice-axe, and if it had been snowing hard she
could even have fashioned a terrific igloo. But fog
was an unknown quantity.

She took a deep breath, refusing to let herself be
cowed. Everything would be just fine, so long as she
kept going in the right direction—and got back safely
before Luke even realised she was missing. She
groaned aloud with that new thought. What he'd do
to her if he ever found out she'd been wandering about
on the fells all alone and in the fog didn't bear thinking
about.

For a while she almost managed to convince herself
she was succeeding, then she jerked in fright as a tree
loomed up at her out of the murk.

'You weren't there before,' she said accusingly,
putting her hand on the rough bark of its strangely
gnarled trunk as though to convince herself it wasn't
just a mirage. 'Dan would have noticed the strange

way you're shaped—he'd have been trying to figure out the best way to silhouette you against a stormy backdrop.'

So she was lost. She pursed her lips grimly, trying to come to terms with the unpalatable fact. What now?

'Seems to me you've got two options, Clancy, girl,' she said, needing to hear the sound of a human voice in the unearthly gloom of the fog. 'You can keep going and risk getting completely lost—or you can find somewhere to hole up till this fog clears.'

Neither option held any appeal, but at last she shrugged her shoulders resignedly, recognising that she didn't really have a choice. If Luke had been there he'd have told her to stay put, to find shelter and safety. And who was she to argue with the advice of an expert? With a sigh of resignation she started to walk on again, praying she'd find a hospitable outcrop of rock somewhere near by. Suddenly the ground seemed to fall away beneath her, and she screamed in sheer terror as she slid helplessly downwards. Landing with a thud on a solid surface, she slowly clambered to her feet, moving tentatively in case she should set off another landslide, then fell back to the ground with a groan as a red-hot pain sliced through her leg.

'Well, you've really done it now, Clancy J. Hall.' Her voice broke on the words. 'This is a fine mess you've gotten yourself into.' She managed to drag herself back against the rock face, manoeuvring her body into the least uncomfortable position she could find. There was nothing she could do now—except wait.

Eternities seemed to pass as she lay sprawled against the ungiving rock, waves of pain washing over her if she attempted to move her injured ankle. She'd managed to unlace her walking-boot, but the agony when she tried to remove it was so intense that she nearly blacked out. Somewhere during the endless wait she felt the stealthy fingers of sleep creeping over her, but she fought their lulling caress, remembering Luke telling her that the body temperature dropped faster in sleep. In a desperate bid to stay awake she began to sing, running through every song in her meagre repertoire several times and finally creating new ones with ridiculous lyrics.

She was in the middle of attempting to sing 'Three Blind Mice' to the tune of Handel's *Messiah*, when the sudden noise of something hurtling down the scree made her jump practically out of her skin.

'What on earth ... ?' Then she gave a great shout of delight as a yellow Labrador, wearing the distinctive red coat of the Search and Rescue Dog Association, bounded up to her, his tail wagging in a frenzy of joy. The animal barked frantically, then rushed headlong off into the gloom, his canine senses untroubled by the fog as he went to alert his handler.

It seemed only seconds later that he reappeared, this time with the unmistakable figure of Luke right behind him.

'Clancy! Dear God, Clancy! Are you all right?' He fell to his knees before her, gathering her into his arms as she sobbed her relief and joy into his shoulder. 'We've been searching for hours. I thought you were dead or seriously injured.' Then he pulled away from

her, his face tautening into grim lines. 'Are you injured?' he asked abruptly.

'Only my ankle, I think. I fell down the scree.
Perhaps I can put my weight on it now.' Leaning on
his arm for support, she slowly began to lever herself
upward. With a faintly sheepish grin she looked up
into his face, too high on sheer happiness to pay any
heed to the threatening storm in his grey eyes. 'How
did you know where to look for me?'

'Your lover told me.'

Shocked by his icy cold clipped tones as much as
by the words themselves, she stared up at him, her
eyes wide and confused.

'My lover? You mean Dan?'

'You have others?' The words seemed torn from
him.

'But Dan isn't my lover! He's my...' She put her
injured foot to the ground, only to scream in agony
as pain engulfed her. As Luke lunged forward to help
her, she fainted clean away in his arms.

CHAPTER ELEVEN

THE journey back to the village remained in Clancy's memory ever afterwards only as a hazy blur, largely because she'd been given a pain-killing shot by the doctor who'd arrived on the scene shortly after Luke. She knew she'd been strapped into some sort of stretcher, had a vague recollection of a large, imposing figure sticking constantly to her side as they made their way down the hillside. Other than that, it could all have been a dream. Until she awoke to find herself in an unfamiliar room.

Alarmed by the clinical atmosphere of the place, she tried to struggle up to a sitting position, only to have a cool, comforting hand laid on her forehead.

'Rest easy now,' a soft voice said somewhere above her ear, and she blinked, trying to focus on the stranger's face.

'Where am I?' To her own surprise she began to giggle weakly. 'Heck, that's an original line.'

A figure in white moved to her side, a friendly smile creasing her features. 'You're in hospital. I've been looking after you since they brought you in.' She shook her head in mock-reproof. 'When that great lunk Luke MacLennan would let me anywhere near you, that is!'

'Luke?' Clancy's forehead creased in a frown as she tried to put together the fragmented pieces of her memory. 'Luke's been here?'

The nurse nodded, smiling slyly as she reached for Clancy's wrist to check her pulse. 'He hasn't left your side since they brought you in. I only managed to persuade him a few minutes ago to go home and get a change of clothes and a shower. I have no doubt he'll be back soon.'

Clancy absorbed the information in silence. Why had Luke stuck to her side so closely? It didn't make sense. Unless he just couldn't wait to bawl her out for her stupidity, of course. That did make sense, and she closed her eyes, her heart sinking at the prospect of yet another showdown. Then she opened them again, looking straight at the nurse.

'Why am I here? I only twisted my ankle.'

The woman shook her head. 'You may have broken it—we can't tell for sure until we've X-rayed it and we can't do that till the swelling goes down. In any case, we like to keep mountain rescue cases in overnight for observation.'

'Has my brother been here?'

'He sure has,' the nurse chuckled richly. 'He was really worried about you, kept blaming himself for leaving you alone. But a certain beautiful blonde helped to put his mind at rest on that score.'

Clancy was seriously beginning to wonder if her brains had been addled in the fall. 'What beautiful blonde?'

'Charlie, of course! Who else? She was with the team that came to find you, and from what I can

gather she was put in charge of reassuring your brother
you were safe and well.' A dimple appeared in her
cheeks as she smiled. 'She's obviously done a good
job—they went off together a while ago, still chat-
tering away like old buddies. Now——' she plumped
up the pillows behind Clancy's head and gave her
shoulder a comforting squeeze '—you get some rest.
The doctor will be in to see you later.'

As the nurse left the room, Clancy gazed about her,
realising she didn't know what time it was—no, strike
that, she thought ruefully; she didn't even know what
day it was. Lying here in this narrow little hospital
bed, she'd never felt more alone or more helpless in
her entire life. She hadn't even felt this bereft on the
fells. Now, on top of everything else, Luke would
probably be even more incensed because her brother
appeared to be interested in Charlie. That was hardly
her fault, of course, but he probably wouldn't see it
that way.

'So you've decided to wake up at last.'

With a feeling of one about to meet her doom,
Clancy looked up into Luke's smoke-grey eyes.

'The nurse said you'd gone home,' she said, then
bit her lip. What a ridiculous and painfully inad-
equate greeting.

'I was intending to. I only made it as far as the
hospital's main door.'

'Then what happened?'

A faint smile creased the corners of his eyes. 'I
realised I couldn't leave until I'd spoken to you.'

She sighed fatalistically. 'Couldn't wait to give me
a good telling-off, you mean.'

'Something like that.'

She gestured to the chair at the side of the bed. 'You might as well have a seat while you're doing it.'

One dark eyebrow quirked quizzically. 'What's wrong, Clancy—can't bear to feel out of control?'

'Something like that.' She smiled wryly, realising she'd just repeated his earlier words.

He took the seat she'd indicated, his eyes never leaving hers as he sat down. She noticed the dark shadow of stubble on his cheeks with a vague feeling of surprise. As rugged as Luke was, she'd never seen him any other way but immaculate—now he looked as if he hadn't slept in a week.

'Then perhaps it'll give you some inkling of how I felt when I realised you were lost somewhere out on the fells—out of my reach and heaven alone knew where.'

She looked away from his probing eyes. 'I know, and I'm sorry. I'd never have stayed up there if I'd realised the weather was about to change so quickly.'

'Well, now you know what it can do.'

She glanced up in surprise. 'Is that it? Is that all you're going to say?'

'You want more?'

She shook her head quickly. 'No. But I thought I was bound to be in for a blistering showdown. I thought you'd really go to town on me for being so stupid.'

'Seems to me you've done that to yourself already.'

She lay back against the pillows, frowning faintly then lifted her hands in a gesture of total bewilderment. 'I just can't win with you,' she said. 'Just when I think I know exactly what to expect—you surprise me all over again.'

He grinned. 'I could say exactly the same about you. But never mind that now. We've got some things to talk about.'

'Such as?' She slanted him a suspicious look.

'Such as . . .' his expression grew serious ' . . . such as the things you were saying as we carried you down the hill.'

She took a sharp intake of breath, scared to even imagine what she might have been saying while under the influence of the pain-killing drug.

'What sort of things?'

He reached for her hand, his fingers warm against hers. 'A lot of it didn't make sense,' he said. 'That's quite normal in the circumstances. But you were talking a lot about a trip abroad. A trip that must have had a profound effect on you, even though you've never even mentioned it to me before.' His eyes seemed to bore into her, searching the shadowed places of her soul. 'Why, Clancy?' he said softly. 'Why have you been bottling all of that up?'

She took a deep shuddering breath, wondering if even now she could bring herself to confide in him. Then she realised she had no real choice. He'd come to her rescue, perhaps even saving her life, and for the second time. The very least she owed him was honesty. 'I couldn't talk about it,' she said at last, her voice low and uneven. 'It went too deep. It hurt too much to see human beings trying to live—no, to exist, in such terrible conditions.'

'You felt guilty.'

Her eyes widened in surprise, then she nodded slowly. 'Did I tell you that?'

'You didn't have to.' He squeezed her hand gently. 'I've been there too.'

'To Sudan?'

He seemed to be looking into the past as he spoke, his eyes darker than normal. 'No. I went to Ethiopia. With a team of relief workers.' For a long moemnt he was silent, his expression set in grim lines. 'I saw people dying like flies all around me. Young people, old people, babies who'd never even had a chance to live. We did what we could, but it didn't even begin to scratch the very surface of the problem. And I felt all the same guilt you've been suffering—guilt because I'd been born into a comparatively wealthy family, guilt because I'd never had to worry about where my next meal was coming from, guilt because I could go home to somewhere very different at the end of it all.'

'How did you deal with it?' Her voice was barely more than a whisper.

'I'm not sure you can ever deal with something like that.' He smiled ruefully. 'I think that's why I gave you such a hard time over not eating properly— because I thought you were hung up on staying slim. I should have recognised you were carrying the same scars I brought home from Ethiopia. And I was the one who told you never to judge a book by its cover!' He shook his head in disgust at his own blindness. 'All you can really do is force people to face up to what's happening over there—talk about it, let them know the hellish reality. Only people can force change, and only then if there's enough of them, speaking with a loud enough voice. That's what your documentary set out to do—and managed it pretty well, too.'

'You know about the documentary?

'Charlie put two and two together after hearing some of the things you were saying. She'd been racking her brains trying to remember where she'd seen your name. Dan confirmed that it had been on the credits of the programme.'

The mention of Charlie's name made Clancy flinch. She looked unhappily away from his eyes. 'About Charlie and Dan,' she began hesitantly.

'Yes? They seem to be getting on extremely well.' He laughed wryly. 'I was getting ready to knock his block off for it.'

She closed her eyes, desperately wishing she were a million miles away. This was it—the moment she'd been dreading all along, the moment when he'd tell her he was in love with Charlie, and probably had been for years. 'I really wouldn't bother about it too much,' she said in a hollow voice. 'Dan's a terrible flirt. But I'm sure Charlie won't take him seriously. Why should she, when she's——?'

'Hang on a minute!' Luke cut her off, his voice sharp with incredulity. 'You've got this all wrong. I was going to knock Dan's block off because I was under the mistaken impression that you and he were lovers, and that he was giving you the run-around. Are you trying to tell me you thought Charlie and I were involved?'

She looked up at him through a haze of confusion. 'You mean you're not?'

His laughter echoed round the small hospital room.
'You sweet dolt! Of course not. Charlie and I have
been friends since we were children—probably about
as close as any two friends can be. But we've never
felt any more for each other than friendship. Probably
because we know each other too well.'

Clancy let out the breath she hadn't even known
she was holding in a sudden rush. 'Oh,' she managed
at last.

'Oh, indeed.' Tenderly he stroked her fringe away
from her forehead and she closed her eyes, weakened
by the sweet warmth of his touch. 'We've both been
getting a lot wrong, haven't we?' he said quietly. 'Me
most of all, first by thinking you were one of those
females who's totally hung up on the way they look,
and the amount they weigh. And secondly by as-
suming that prickly exterior of yours was genuine.'

'What makes you think it isn't?'

A warm glow lit his eyes from within. 'Because I
know now that you were simply trying to shield a soft
and vulnerable heart from further pain. Your
brother's put me straight on quite a lot about you.
Did you know he's your biggest fan?' He grinned
broadly. 'Mind you, he also cruised very close to the
wind for a while there.'

'Dan did? How?'

'By realising I'd mistakenly assumed he was your
lover. And by pretending for a while that it was true—
he really played on it too, all the time he was with me
in the office supposedly discussing the mountain
rescue shoot.'

She frowned uncomprehendingly. 'I don't understand. Why would he do such a thing?'

'Because he thought he could make me jealous.'

And much good it had done, she thought ruefully,
gazing into the face of the man she'd come to love so
deeply, despite all her most strenuous efforts to resist.
Soon she'd be leaving this place—and this man—and
the pain of it would be greater than anything she'd
ever known.

'You must thank Charlie and all the others who
came to find me,' she blurted out, suddenly afraid
that the emotion welling up within her must surely
burst through the crumbling walls of her defences.
When he looked at her like that, with such exquisite
tenderness, it was almost possible to imagine he cared
for her too, but she'd be lost forever if she allowed
herself to believe it for a split-second.

'You can tell them yourself.'

She shook her head abruptly. 'I don't want to see
them,' she said. 'They must think I'm a real idiot.'

He chuckled softly. 'I think you'll find they're very
forgiving of human frailties. Heaven knows, we encounter them often enough.'

'Even so,' she argued stubbornly, 'I'd prefer to leave
the hospital and go home without any fuss.'

To her surprise he nodded. 'Good idea. I'll be able
to keep an eye on you there.'

'Keep an eye on me?' Her expression was a picture
of sheer confusion. 'In my home?'

'No. In mine.'

'But I'm not going...'

'Yes, you are.' There was a glint of humour in his dark eyes but his tone was uncompromising. 'When you leave here, which should be in a couple of days, you're coming home with me.'

For a couple of blissful moments she allowed herself the fantasy of imagining what it would be like. Then she firmly shut the picture out of her mind. She had to leave some time, and it could only be all the more agonising if she'd been in his home, shared his space, learned even more about him. 'Look, it's really kind of you to suggest it, but there's no need. I won't be alone if that's what you're concerned about. I'll ask a friend to help out while I'm still hobbling about.'

'Clancy J. Hall, you're a stubborn creature.'

She eyed him suspiciously, wondering what was coming next. 'Yes?'

'But you've met your match. So save yourself the effort of arguing, because it's all settled. You're coming home with me, and that's final.'

'I won't!' Desperation raised her voice an octave as she stared back at him. 'Don't you see? I can't!'

'Why not?'

'Because I might never want to leave.' She bit her lip hard, horrified to hear her own voice betraying her that way. The words had been reverberating in her mind, but she'd never intended to say them.

'Good,' he returned calmly. 'Because I fully intend never to let you leave.'

'What? I don't understand...'

'No, you don't, you sweet, silly fool.' Shaking his head in affectionate amusement, he took her hand in

both of his. 'In my admittedly rather ham-fisted way
I'm asking you to stay, Clancy. With me. Forever.'

'But why?'

'Isn't it obvious?' The warmth in his eyes reached
out to her, enfolding her like a possessive embrace.
'I love you, Clancy. And don't try telling me you don't
love me right back, because I know you do. You told
me so on the way down the mountainside.'

'I did? Oh, hell! But that doesn't mean...you don't
have to...what I mean is...'

'Shut up, Clancy,' he said tenderly. 'If you're attempting to say I don't have to feel responsible for
you—I don't. At least, not in the way you mean.' He
smiled wryly. 'Though perhaps I should. You've been
driving me crazy ever since the first time I saw you
weaving about on the road, half asleep at the wheel.
You lodged yourself right into my heart and you refused to be budged. But I only really faced up to the
truth of how I feel about you when your blasted
brother managed to drive me half crazy with jealousy.
When I discovered you were missing on the fells, I
nearly went insane to think I could have lost you
forever. So you see—you have to stay.'

'Well, if you put it that way...' She looked up at
him with sparkling eyes, joy spreading like a warm
ray of sunshine throughout her entire soul, sweeping
away all the doubts, uncertainties and heartaches of
the past. Then she frowned. 'But what about the
company? Dan and I are partners. I couldn't just leave
him in the lurch.'

'I wouldn't ask you to,' Luke said. 'And, despite
all your claims to the contrary, I'm not really as much

of a chauvinist as you seem to think. I think you should stay with the company—your work's obviously important to you and you're good at it, judging by the famine documentary. But you don't have to be based in London, surely?'

Her smile returned full measure. 'You're right. I don't. Oh, Luke . . .' Emotion welled up within her as she gazed into his eyes, barely able to believe all that was happening. 'You really love me?'

'I really do,' he returned solemnly.

'And I love you. Oh, so very much. I always will.'

'You'd better,' he growled tenderly as he took her carefully but firmly into his arms. 'Or you might just see me turn into a caveman all over again.'

She turned her head to seek his kiss, and it seemed her very heart was singing within her. Luke hadn't just rescued her from the swimming-pool and from the fells, she realised with a deep sensation of joy. He'd rescued her from herself and all the shadows of pain she'd been carrying. With this man her heart would be safe forever.

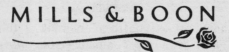

4 FREE

Romances and 2 FREE gifts just for you!

You can enjoy all the heartwarming emotion of true love for FREE! Discover the heartbreak and happiness, the emotion and the tenderness of the modern relationships in Mills & Boon Romances.

We'll send you 4 Romances as a special offer from Mills & Boon Reader Service, along with the opportunity to have 6 captivating new Romances delivered to your door each month.

Claim your FREE books and gifts overleaf...

An irresistible offer from Mills & Boon

Become a regular reader of Romances with Mills & Boon Reader Service and we'll welcome you with 4 books, a CUDDLY TEDDY and a special MYSTERY GIFT all absolutely FREE.

And then look forward to receiving 6 brand new Romances each month, delivered to your door hot off the presses, postage and packing FREE! Plus our free Newsletter featuring author news, competitions, special offers and much more.

This invitation comes with no strings attached. You may cancel or suspend your subscription at any time, and still keep your free books and gifts.

It's so easy. Send no money now. Simply fill in the coupon below and post it to -
Reader Service, FREEPOST, PO Box 236, Croydon, Surrey CR9 9EL.

NO STAMP REQUIRED

Free Books Coupon

Yes! Please rush me 4 FREE Romances and 2 FREE gifts! Please also reserve me a Reader Service subscription. If I decide to subscribe I can look forward to receiving 6 brand new Romances for just £10.80 each month, postage and packing FREE. If I decide not to subscribe I shall write to you within 10 days - I can keep the free books and gifts whatever I choose. I may cancel or suspend my subscription at any time. I am over 18 years of age.

Ms/Mrs/Miss/Mr _____ EP56R

Address _____

_____

Postcode _____ Signature _____

MAILING PREFERENCE SERVICE

Next Month's Romances

Each month you can choose from a wide variety of romance with Mills & Boon. Below are the new titles to look out for next month, why not ask either Mills & Boon Reader Service or your Newsagent to reserve you a copy of the titles you want to buy – just tick the titles you would like and either post to Reader Service or take it to any Newsagent and ask them to order your books.

Please save me the following titles:	**Please tick**	**√**
A DIFFICULT MAN	Lindsay Armstrong	
MARRIAGE IN JEOPARDY	Miranda Lee	
TENDER ASSAULT	Anne Mather	
RETURN ENGAGEMENT	Carole Mortimer	
LEGACY OF SHAME	Diana Hamilton	
A PART OF HEAVEN	Jessica Marchant	
CALYPSO'S ISLAND	Rosalie Ash	
CATCH ME IF YOU CAN	Anne McAllister	
NO NEED FOR LOVE	Sandra Marton	
THE FABERGE CAT	Anne Weale	
AND THE BRIDE WORE BLACK	Helen Brooks	
LOVE IS THE ANSWER	Jennifer Taylor	
BITTER POSSESSION	Jenny Cartwright	
INSTANT FIRE	Liz Fielding	
THE BABY CONTRACT	Suzanne Carey	
NO TRESPASSING	Shannon Waverly	

If you would like to order these books in addition to your regular subscription from Mills & Boon Reader Service please send £1.80 per title to: Mills & Boon Reader Service, Freepost, P.O. Box 236, Croydon, Surrey, CR9 9EL, quote your Subscriber No:.................................... (If applicable) and complete the name and address details below. Alternatively, these books are available from many local Newsagents including W.H.Smith, J.Menzies, Martins and other paperback stockists from 8 October 1993.

Name:..

Address:..

....Post Code:........................

To Retailer: If you would like to stock M&B books please contact your regular book/magazine wholesaler for details.